while you were gone

DUPLEXITY, PART II

Also by Amy K. Nichols

now that you're here

DUPLEXITY, PART I

while you were gone

DUPLEXITY, PART II

AMY K. NICHOLS

ALFRED A. KNOPF 　 NEW YORK

FOR Z. AND C.

do one thing every day that scares you

THIS IS A BORZOI BOOK PUBLISHED BY ALFRED A. KNOPF

All rights reserved. Published in the United States by Alfred A. Knopf, an imprint of Random House Children's Books, a division of Penguin Random House LLC, New York.

Knopf, Borzoi Books, and the colophon are registered trademarks of Penguin Random House LLC.

Visit us on the Web! randomhouseteens.com

Educators and librarians, for a variety of teaching tools, visit us at RHTeachersLibrarians.com

Library of Congress Cataloging-in-Publication Data
Nichols, Amy.
While you were gone / Amy K. Nichols. — First edition.
pages cm. — (Duplexity ; part 2)
Summary: Eevee, an aspiring artist and daughter of Arizona's governor, and Danny, a reformed troublemaker who lives in foster care in his own world, join forces to correct a breach between parallel universes.
ISBN 978-0-385-75392-0 (trade) — ISBN 978-0-385-75393-7 (lib. bdg.) — ISBN 978-0-385-75394-4 (ebook)
[1. Space and time—Fiction. 2. Identity—Fiction. 3. Artists—Fiction. 4. Science fiction.] I. Title.
PZ7.N527Whi 2015
[Fic]—dc23
2014042558

The text of this book is set in 11.5-point Requiem.

Printed in the United States of America
August 2015
10 9 8 7 6 5 4 3 2 1

First Edition

1

EEVEE

I used to think the two scariest words in the English language were *the* and *end.* As in, finished. Over. Dead and gone.

I was wrong.

The two scariest words are *what* and *if.* As in, what if I'm not good enough? What if the answer is no? What if they're watching? What if I get caught? What if everyone finds out? What if no one cares?

What if this is all there is?

What. If.

2

Danny

The slamming door sends a thousand sound-shards through my brain. I steady myself against the garbage can. Stupid hangover. When the ringing stops, I flip my hair out of my eyes and scuff across the yard, shoes kicking up dust and bits of dead grass. My hair falls back in my face, but I leave it. Sun's too bright. Every step feels like metal scraping up the bones of my neck.

Behind me, the engine of Brent's work truck growls to life. He revs a couple times before backing out of the driveway, but I just keep walking, eyes forward, putting one foot in front of the other. Every day, we play this game. Who flinches first? When the engine's so loud my head's gonna explode, I turn around to face him.

A roar of sound rushes at me. He lays on the horn. Tires take over the sidewalk.

Come on. Hit me. Mow me down.

But the truck swerves, bounces as it lumbers back into

the street. The loose muffler swings, belching blue exhaust. Brent flips me off, guns the engine and speeds away. I watch until he's out of sight, then listen until the engine is gone, too.

One day he'll do it. But not today.

At the end of the street, I turn the corner and the sun hits me full in the face. I grope through my jacket pockets, but my sunglasses must be back at the house. No way I'm going there again until I have to. I take cover under a tree, pull out a pack of smokes instead and light one up. My head rushes with the first drag. I lean against the block wall and wait for the pain to go away.

A car drives by. A dog barks. I keep my eyes closed. Breathe. Wonder what would happen if I just disappeared.

It would get me out of school, for starters.

Suzy's words whisper into my thoughts. *If you ditch again, they'll suspend you. And don't think for a second he won't find out.*

Last time attendance called, Brent pinned me down and pressed that damn cigar into my arm. The others ran to their rooms. They knew better than to hang around. Later, Benny wouldn't come near me. Said I scared him. That I sounded like an angry dog. It took two days for him to talk to me again, even though I told him over and over I wasn't mad. Not at him, at least.

It's bad enough us older fosters have to live in that place, but a little guy like Ben? That's just not right. None of this is.

I suck down the last of the cigarette and flick the stub into the gravel. Better get a move on or I'll have to face Brent again, and his cigar.

Class has already started by the time I get to school. Ms. Fischbach glares when I open the door, and everyone watches me walk to the only empty desk. Everyone except the dark-haired girl who sits next to me. My shoes squeak on the linoleum, so I make the trek long and drawn out. *Squeak. Squeak.* When I flop into my chair, the girl looks over, then back down at her notebook. She's always drawing stuff.

"Turn to page 774 in your anthology." Ms. Fischbach's mouth is wide like a frog's, and her voice makes my ears bleed. If I put my head on the desk and fold my arms around, I can almost block out the noise. There's still the shuffle of backpacks and the thud of books landing on desks. That kid with the stutter starts reading. He's like a car engine that won't turn. I squeeze my arms tighter around. My breath sounds like ocean waves. I feel myself fading. . . .

Out of nowhere, cold grips my chest, freezing me from the inside, and a freight train roars through my ears. I can't breathe. Stars swirl in my eyes. I try to lift my head, but I'm pinned. The floor shifts and is gone. With it the desk, the chair, the room. I claw and kick at the force pulling me down, but there's nothing to fight against.

So I let go. Let my body fall. Give myself up to the dark.

3

EEVEE

Vivian's words gnaw at me the entire ride.

I'm applying to Belford, too. Bosca says I stand a chance.

Nothing shakes them—not the music Jonas plays on the car radio, not the stop-and-go traffic, not even downtown rising into view. As he pulls into the Tower complex, they crowd around so close I actually raise my hand to swat them away. I wish I could swat her away, too.

Jonas leaves the engine running as he walks around to open my door. He reaches in to take my book bag.

I place a hand on it. "It's okay. I've got this one."

He nods and goes to the trunk for my suitcase. I step out of the car and bump the door with my hip, hoping I've shut Vivian's voice inside.

Nope. *You're not the only artist at this school, you know.*

What if she gets in and I don't? What if we *both* end up in Edinburgh? What if they assign us to be *roommates?*

Jonas sets my suitcase on the curb. I shift the book bag strap on my shoulder. "Thanks."

He doffs an imaginary cap and returns to the car. I walk inside and the door closes behind me, sealing me in the Sniffer. Three blasts of air move my skirt and mess up my hair. I exhale and wait through swishing and clicking sounds as the machine analyzes if I'm safe or not. Finally, I get the green light. The Sniffer chamber opens and I'm allowed into the elevator. I press 14 and face my reflection.

Of course I'll get into Belford. I'm Eevee Solomon.

The girl staring back at me doesn't look so sure. My bags fall to the floor and I turn around, holding on to the rail with both hands. The cameras are watching but I don't care.

Does Vivian have to infringe on *every* part of my life? Ever since her dad challenged mine for the governorship, she's been trying to outdo me at everything. She followed me to Kierland Academy, switched to fine arts, weaseled her way into Bosca's master studio. Now she wants to apply for a Belford internship? I doubt she even knew where Scotland was before I mentioned it.

If only I hadn't screwed everything up going down to the vaults. What was I thinking?

I take a deep breath and turn around to look at my reflection. Straighten my shoulders and smooth my hair. Rummage through my bag and apply a fresh coat of Stormy Pink.

I've got this. My jury exhibit will blow everyone away. The public will rave about my paintings. I'll be Bosca's star student again. Belford will beg me to apply. By this time next year, I'll be shining so bright no one will even remember Vivian Hayes, that nobody girl who thought she could be me.

The elevator slows to a stop and the doors open. Smiling,

I pick up my bags and walk down the hallway, passing paintings depicting Arizona's history. Arrival of the first settlers. Migrant farmers in citrus groves. Native American tribesmen on horseback. The Battle of Cabeza Prieta. I slip into the East Room, set my bags down and close the doors behind me. The dull light of morning filters through open windows. A vase of spider mums sits on the baby grand. I check the clock on the mantel. Jonas arrived early this morning to pick me up. Twenty minutes to wait now, if Richard has everything running on schedule.

I sweep my fingers across the piano's glossy finish before sitting on the bench and resting them on the keys. Mom used to play in college, but that was a long time ago. As far as I know, I'm the only person who ever touches this beauty. And that's only on weekends when I'm staying here with my parents instead of on campus. They have pianos in the practice rooms at school, but good luck finding one empty. And the music students get angry when nonprogram students invade their space. Can't blame them, I guess. I'd get pretty cranky if I found some trumpet player taking up residence in the art studio.

Winston's "February Sea" begins with soft, slow arpeggios and a repeating low G. I always start quiet, afraid of breaking the silence. As if anyone will hear me. The bedrooms are on the opposite side of the Tower, with too many boardrooms between to count. Seven measures in, I press the keys harder, letting the melody fill the room. The notes run through my brain like miles of familiar road. Scenery I no longer see. My brain slips into autopilot and Vivian's words whisper in the spaces between the notes. When I close my eyes, I see her gloating smile.

If only I could go back and change the night of Bosca's exhibit. That was when the power shifted, when, like an idiot, I handed Vivian the ammo to use against me. I should have known better than to go down to see the Retrogressives. Mom always said my impulsiveness would be my downfall. I hate when she's right.

My fingers pound the keys, sending shudders through the piano.

This is probably just one of Bosca's wacky plans, encouraging her to apply for the internship and Belford. Promoting Vivian is his way of keeping me on track. Not because she's actually his new prize student or anything. There's just no way.

When my fingers begin to ache from the punishment, I switch gears, running quieter patterns in the upper registers while my brain runs through the day ahead. Richard will retrieve me and we'll scurry off—not a minute to waste—to Conference Room B for debrief. Then, fashionably late, the governor will barge in with all the bluster of a tornado. Christine will follow, tablet and stylus at the ready. The governor will bark orders at Richard, then place both hands on the table before moving his gaze over to where I stand behind the second chair to his left. I'll see wariness in his eyes, but then he'll smile at me and I'll kiss him on the cheek and say, "Hello, Daddy," like a good daughter should.

The bridge races beneath my fingers, punctuated by accents and trills.

He'll ask about school and I'll tell him what he wants to

hear. Both of us will ignore the uncomfortable stuff. Later today, he and Mom and I will travel together over to the stadium and make our appearance at the Patriot Day celebration. We'll wave. We'll smile. We'll leave.

Approaching the coda, the music slows, and my fingers press the keys with care, each note growing quieter than the one before.

Will Vivian be at the celebration, too?

My shoulders slump. The arpeggios slow to a stop. My mind is blank. I stare at the vase's reflection before starting six measures back, playing the low arpeggios leading into the transition. At the same spot, my fingers stop again.

I look at my hands like it's their fault I can't remember the next chord, let alone the next note. Suspended sixth? No. Repeat of the bridge? That isn't right either.

The last, wrong chord hangs in the air, the keys pinned down by my fingers. The room is so still even the dust motes float motionless in the window's light.

The floor trembles and the water in the vase ripples. I lift my hands and listen, fingers hovering just above the keys. Above me the chandelier sways.

The floor trembles again and this time the piano strings whisper a ghostly moan. Chills run up my arms. My foot slips from the sustain pedal. Far off, I hear sirens.

Then footsteps. Not Richard's long strides, but hurried, staccato ones. Both doors bang open and two security guys swoop into the room.

"Miss Solomon," the big one says, taking my elbow. The other speaks into his wrist: "Sparrow in the East Room." In a rush of movement, I'm out the door, half carried down fourteen flights of stairs. Fluorescent lights and floor numbers blur past: 12, 10, 7, 4. By the time the basement bunker doors open, I'm dizzy and my heart pounds a fierce rhythm in my ears.

4

Danny

The darkness spits me out, hurtling me through a rush of light and sound. The ground breaks my fall and I shatter in an explosion of pain.

And silence.

Fingers press against my neck. I squint open my eyes.

A cop kneels over me. His lips move, but I can't hear him. Can't hear anything. My hands claw the pavement. Where am I? He talks into a radio and motions for me to stay. Faces move in and out of view. More hands reach under me, lifting me up from the ground. Gray sky and swirling ash fill my eyes before everything bleeds away to white.

5

EEVEE

My hands won't stop moving. My fingers wring around each other, curl into fists, press flat against my jeans and curl into fists again. Mom stills them with her own firm hand and gives a quick shake of her head. *Stop.* I look over at Dad, sitting on the other couch. His face is serious but composed.

Some moments are bigger than others. They weigh more. They stop you in your tracks. When you're in one, somehow you know: This is going to matter, so pay attention.

Like when Dad was sworn in as governor. Watching him raise his hand and repeat the oath, I had this feeling, this knowing, that nothing would ever be the same again.

It's the feeling I have now.

Images flash on the wall of monitors. Ash and smoke. A tattered Arizona flag. Soldiers and security and everyday people helping each other sort through the chaos. Three screens broadcast the latest news reports, a bank of black-and-whites displays live Spectrum security feeds from the site of the attack, two monitors wait on standby for incoming communications, and one shows Barcelona winning three to zip.

"Another," Richard says, swiping a finger across his tablet. "Death toll at four."

"Wearing a hole in the carpet won't change that," Dad says. "Sit down."

Richard sits on the arm of the couch because he does what Dad tells him to do. It doesn't stop him from checking for updates, though. His hair is turning gray at the temples. It'll be white by the time he's done serving as Dad's chief of staff. "Christine sent the draft of your public statement."

He passes Dad the tablet, then turns up the volume on the news. A reporter stands a safe distance from a military blockade. Behind her, smoke rises from the rubble that used to be Port Royale Way. South of where she's standing is Jansen Fine Arts Services, where my work is getting prepped for installation. My hands escape their lockdown and I chew on my thumbnail before Mom stops them again.

"Power is still out for thousands as crews continue to search for survivors. Though the investigation is ongoing, an anonymous government official said a terrorist-detonated EMP is suspected—"

Dad hands the tablet back to Richard. "Tell Christine this needs more grit. People need to understand the dangers they face."

"They?"

"*We*. More inspiration, too." He stands and stretches. "We're in this together," he says in his speech-giving voice. "We'll get through if we all work toward a stable society. There is no room for those who . . ." His voice fades as he and Richard disappear into the kitchen. Mom picks up the remote and mutes the TV.

One of the monitors flashes a spinning graphic—PATRIOT DAY PANIC—as the news ticker scrolls across the bottom. The screen shows a replay of the explosion, caught by Spectrum. A rising plume of smoke fills the view from across the mall parking lot. People duck and scatter in every direction. The camera shakes and debris flies as the second blast hits. The whole thing plays again in slow motion. It's surreal watching with the sound off. Makes it feel like it's happening somewhere far away. Makes me realize how quiet it is down here, cut off from all the people and noise.

Mom lets go of my hands and pats me on the knee. "Don't worry. We're safe."

The last time we were in the bunker, I was a moody twelve-year-old, annoyed that I had to get off the phone to go underground. That was when Red December blew up the light-rail tracks over by Goldwater Field and turned downtown into a total mess. It never crossed my mind that something bad could have actually happened to us that day. With the concrete barricades and closed-off streets around the Executive Tower, it seemed impossible anyone could get close enough to try.

I don't know if it's me that's changed or the world, but this seems worse. Bigger. Closer to home.

This time people weren't just inconvenienced. People died.

I close my eyes but still see the images in my mind. "I'll be back," I mumble as I walk to my room—well, the room that's considered mine down here in the bunker. I leave the door cracked a smidge so I can hear what's going on in the main living space, and fish my book bag out from where I stashed it under the bed. After a quick check to make sure the coast is still clear, I sit with my back against the wall, the door almost closed beside me. My hand slips inside the bag and pulls out the slim hardback book. Its corners are worn with age and from me lugging it around, no doubt. The title is scratched up, too, stamped gold against the plain black cover. *Retrogressive.*

I know my fascination with the paintings is wrong, and that there's something not right with my brain that draws me to them, but I can't help it.

I open the book and my fingers navigate past the flyleaves and long-winded introduction. They know the way; they've done this countless times. The pages are thick and glossy. I flip through until I find the artist that fits: Pablo Picasso. As my eyes take in the feast of line and shape, my hands go quiet, my shoulders relax. I let the painting fill my mind until it's all I can see and the ugliness out there is erased by this beautiful chaos instead. My finger traces the progression of angles and shadows down to the words. My lips form them silently. *Ma Jolie.* My pretty girl.

If anyone saw me with this, if anyone knew my secret—

Vivian.

I turn from Picasso over to Ramsey. The faces in his *Iterations* laugh, scream, cry. I haven't looked at this one since the night of Bosca's exhibit. I haven't been brave enough. Seeing them now brings a flood of emotions. Fear. Anger. Regret.

Deconstructing Complacency was set to be the event of the year. The Department of Public Compliance had lifted curfew the day before and people were itching to get out and live again. The line to get into the museum wrapped clear around the building and stretched all the way down to McDowell Road. This was big-time. And Bosca had put me in charge.

He was in rare form, making demands left and right. Being lead intern, I took the brunt of his drama. The others did whatever they could just to stay away. As the clock ticked down to opening, Bosca got snippy. When he demanded to see the museum director for the hundredth time, I asked Vivian to go instead. Twenty minutes to opening, I still needed to change my clothes and fix my hair. She stormed off, muttering under her breath, resentful that I'd given her something to do. I blew her off, grabbed my things and headed to the restroom.

I slipped into my dress—a red, strappy design I'd been dying for an excuse to wear—and tried to get myself fancied up. Even with hair pinned up and perfect lipstick, I looked stressed. My forehead was etched with worry and my hands wouldn't stop moving.

So instead of returning to the green room, I took the stairs down to the vaults. I knew it was a risk, but I had a few minutes and my feet led the way. With the museum closed and all the Bosca action happening upstairs, the hallways below were empty. Still, I tried to keep my heels quiet as I walked across the concrete floor toward the storage room at the far end. Unlike the passcode-protected vaults full of prized works of art, the reject room's door is never locked.

It's small and crowded in there. I crept around the statue of the man with stick-thin arms and inched past the paintings stacked against the baseboards. Crouching down, I flipped through them. Some are framed, some are just raw canvas. Others are rolled up and stand on end in the corner. I've never taken time to investigate those. Whatever they are, like all the other pieces stuffed in the room, they've been labeled Retrogressive, unfit for society. They're dragged out from time to time to be shown as cautionary examples of disorder, illness, depravity, and then put away again for fear of corrupting minds.

That night, I stopped on Ramsey's *Iterations,* a collage of faces exhibiting a range of emotions. Dread, sadness, joy. Rather than disorder, my mind filled with a sense of wonder, a sense of ease, just as it had the other times I'd snuck down there.

"Eevee?"

I pushed the paintings away with a gasp.

Vivian made a disgusted face. "What are you doing in *here*?"

"I—"

She crossed her arms as the disgust turned to a sly grin. "Caught ya, didn't I?"

My hands fell limp at my sides. She raised an eyebrow and turned, saying, "What will Bosca think of his little star now?"

Bosca was angry. Dismayed. He promoted Vivian to lead intern and put me on provisional status.

My parents don't know. Yet.

Which is why I have to make sure the work I present to the jury is acceptable. Not only so I can prove that I'm a good artist and upstanding citizen, but also so I can go somewhere else, like Belford, a place where I wouldn't be considered different, weird or disgraceful.

Dad passes by outside. "We need to make them realize it's for their own good."

My hand braces against the door. The other grips the book.

A second set of footsteps—Richard's—follows. "They'll get on board. Trust me. The hardest part of all this will be the cleanup."

"When do we get to go back upstairs?" Mom asks.

"Soon." Dad's voice moves from one side of the room to the other. "They have to make sure the complex is secure first. Where's Eve?"

"I think it was too much for her."

"Yes, well . . ." Dad's voice turns to a mumble and I can't make out what he says or Mom's response. The knock on the door startles me. "Eve?"

My hands fumble as they shove the book back into the bag. The door begins to swing and I press against it with my knee. Too hard. It bangs shut.

"Everything okay?"

"Yes." I scramble across the floor and slide the bag back under the bed. "Hang on." A swipe of my foot and the strap disappears under the dust ruffle. I brush off my jeans and smooth my hair. By the time I open the door, Dad's over by Mom again. They stop midconversation and stare at me. Richard looks up from his tablet, too. Behind them, the images of the attack flicker across the monitors. "I was . . ." My hands resume their fidgeting.

Mom opens her mouth to say something to me but turns to Dad instead. "You were saying?"

Richard looks back down at his tablet. Dad picks up the remote. "I'm afraid we're down here until security decides we're safe."

"Well, I wish they'd hurry," Mom says with a sigh. "I just want everything to go back to normal."

"It will." Dad turns up the volume on Barcelona. "It always does."

6

Danny

Next thing I know, I'm lying on a tarp under a tree with the world imploding around me. Sirens scream. Smoke chokes the air. People stumble past. Beside me, a woman holds a bloody cloth to her head. Beyond her, medics load a gurney into the back of an ambulance. Everything is loud and hot and close. And none of it is familiar.

I push myself up and see my own hands wrapped in gauze. What happened? I close my eyes and think back.

I dodged Brent's truck. Walked to school. Grabbed a quick smoke before going to class. Got there late—

A slamming door makes me jump. The ambulance bounds over the curb and its siren wails. A woman crouches in front of me. "Welcome back." Her smile is grim. She unslings the stethoscope from around her neck and presses it against my chest. Holds two fingers on my wrist to check my pulse.

These aren't my clothes. "Where's my jacket?"

She shakes her head and puts the stethoscope back around

her neck. Pulls a penlight from her pocket and flashes it over my eyes. "That's your sweatshirt behind you, isn't it? We used it for a pillow. Dizzy?"

"No."

"Pain anywhere?"

"Chest feels tight."

"Asthma?" she asks.

I shake my head.

"Probably reacting to all the soot in the air."

"What's wrong with my hands?"

"Superficial lacerations. Compliance officer said you were climbing a fence when the bomb went off. You got scraped up pretty good when you landed. Lucky nothing's broken." She taps my knees and elbows with the side of the penlight. "I'd send you over to Harbor Samaritan, but they're full up. What's your name?"

"Danny."

"Did you come here with anyone, Danny?"

I shake my head.

"Officers are working on contacting your family. Hang tight." She pats me on the knee and goes to help a woman with a cut on her leg hobbling toward the tarp.

I lift the gauze to look at my palms. Road rash. Fingers scraped up, but nothing too—

What the—?

I hold my arms out in front of me. They should be covered in red-pink scars from Brent's cigar. But—

Everything blurs. The people, the noise. It melts away until all I see is me.

I stretch my fingers wide. The scars are gone. The calluses, too. And my long hair. I've never seen these clothes before, not even the sweatshirt the nurse said was mine. The world around me moves in slow motion.

Think, Ogden. You walked in late to English. Sat in your chair. Put your head down and fell asleep.

Fell.

I fell. There was darkness and a pulling. Then the floor was gone and I fell through. I thought I was dying. But I didn't die.

I landed.

Here.

And the scars are gone.

Someone calls my name. I look up through the sea of people. When I hear it again, I push myself up to stand. A cop walks toward me, the same one I saw before. His mouth is a thin line, his eyes searching. He stops to let a person in a wheelchair pass, then sees me and nods. He motions behind him for someone to follow. I try to see past him but there are too many—

"Whoa there." A medic catches me.

"S'okay." I shake my head and free my arm. Beyond the cop, a tall man in sunglasses walks into view. He holds out his hand to the woman on his right.

It can't be.

I take a step, sure the ground won't be there, and trip over the woman with the bleeding head. "Sorry." I don't stop. I just keep walking toward them and they keep walking toward me until the space between us is gone and we're standing face to face. I open my mouth to speak but nothing comes out.

My parents are dead. I watched their coffins go into the ground.

Mom wraps her arms around me. "Oh, Danny. We thought we'd lost you."

7

EEVEE

Early Friday evening, we're finally released from our confinement. Taking the elevator from the bunker all the way to the top floor feels like being reborn. Dad retreats to his office. I stop to look out over the city before joining Mom in the kitchen. She goes on and on about how good it is to be back upstairs, how we all must be starving, how she doesn't understand why some people refuse to integrate into society. Meanwhile, I prepare green beans. When she's said all she can say about the bad things in the world, she starts in on me wanting to study abroad.

"It's so far away," she says, flipping the tilapia fillets. "Why not choose something closer?"

I think the things I can't say: *Because* it's far away and because over *there* they don't censor art. But what I say to her is, "Because it's the best."

"Well, your father and I still aren't convinced."

Gripping the knife, I pulverize the beans.

"How about we see if you get in and then decide?"

I'm so annoyed I can't answer. In fact, I don't say anything the rest of the time we're in the kitchen, or after we've gotten dinner ready.

The dining table is ridiculously long for a family of three, but necessary for dinners with dignitaries. Mom and I sit across from each other at one end, waiting for Dad to join us. He's always on the phone. Just part of the job when you're the gov. Mom turns pages in a manila folder beside her plate. She's always reading boring papers and proposals. Just part of the job when you're a lobbyist. A candle sits on the table, its light competing with the chandelier overhead. I watch the flame's reflection in the window overlooking Phoenix. The city stretches out in a shimmering grid of gold and silver lights. It's beautiful. But the darkness hides an ugly truth: Part of the city is without power. A mall lies in smoldering ruins. That's on the other side of the Executive Tower, though, so we don't have to think about it while we eat. Out of sight, out of mind.

"We need to go shopping," Mom says, breaking the silence but not looking up from her work. "Governor's Gala is just around the corner."

The thought feels like grit in my mouth. "They're still going to have it? Even with everything going on?"

"Of course," she says. "It's a tradition. I think you should go with Chad. He's a nice kid."

"Mom, I told you before—"

Dad's entrance rescues me from having to explain for the thousandth time that I don't want to go with Chad to the gala, or anywhere, ever. "Fine. Keep me posted." He tucks his phone into his pocket, opens the media cabinet on the wall and turns on the flat screen. President Coradetti stands at a podium, a flag-lined hallway behind him. His face is stern.

". . . because what happened in Phoenix could happen any-where. The truth is, there are forces strategizing against our great nation. Individuals and organizations actively plotting to harm our people. They are ruthless. They are heart—" The lights flicker and the television glitches.

"What was that?" Mom asks.

"Fluctuation in the power grid," Dad says, waving his hand to quiet her. "It's to be expected."

The president unfreezes. ". . . will not stop until they've unraveled the very fabric of our society. We cannot and will not let that happen. I am working closely with Governor Solomon and security agencies to ensure the safety and well-being of the good people of Arizona. We will move through this dark and dangerous time toward a better tomorrow, but only if we stand together and stand strong. Thank you." The presidential seal fills the screen before it returns to regular news.

Dad mutes the TV and sits at the head of the table. I watch the reporter's lips move, waiting for the lights to flicker again. Dad sighs. "How am I going to follow that speech?"

"You're going to be great." Mom puts a hand on his shoulder.

"I just don't think anyone realizes the pressure. . . ."

"You were made for times like this. And we'll be right there to support you. Right, Eve?"

Behind her, scenes of military personnel and cleanup crews

move across the screen. I force myself to smile. "Of course. You've got this."

He smiles. "Where would I be without my girls? Is this creole tilapia? You must really love me." He winks at Mom and digs in. My own fish remains untouched. I push it around a little with my fork.

"Eve," he says, his face and emotions back in check, "I received word that school is no longer on lockdown. Jonas can take you back straight from the press conference tomorrow."

I exhale. Loud.

"Yes, yes, we know," he says. "You can't wait to get away."

"Security will be on alert?" Mom's voice is tense.

"What kind of father would I be if I didn't look out for my daughter when terrorists threaten to undermine the safety of our city?"

"Is that from tomorrow's speech?"

"You could tell?"

"Maybe a little less dramatic with the delivery." She dabs her mouth with her napkin. "Eve and I were discussing the gala. We need to find dresses."

"And a date."

"Well, I know who I'm going with." She pats his arm.

"What's the name of that intern in your office? Charlie?"

"Chad," Mom says.

"Good kid." He sips from his water glass. "Eve should go with him."

I blurt out, "I'm not going."

That gets their attention.

"Of course you are," Mom says. "Don't be ridiculous."

"Ridiculous?" I point my fork at the TV. "You're talking about dresses when someone just attacked the city, and *I'm* the one being ridiculous?"

"Eve." Dad's voice is low. Mom and I both ignore him.

"There are traditions," she says, "and standards you don't appreciate—"

"I have deadlines you don't appreciate."

"We're all busy."

"The Art Guild jury is the same day as the gala. I'll be up to my eyeballs in preparations."

She crosses her arms. "What will people think if you're not there?"

"I don't care what people think."

"Enough!" Dad slams his knife down on the table. The candle flame dances. "You're going to the gala and that's that."

"What about my art?"

"Your art," Mom says. "That's all you ever think about. Do you ever stop to consider what's best for our family?"

Dad takes a deep breath. "Girls, there's enough drama going on out there, we don't need more of it in here. Eve, I don't care if you go with Chad or Charlie or some schmo off the street. You'll be at the gala and you'll be on your best behavior."

Mom rests her hands in her lap and raises an eyebrow.

He picks up his knife and fork. "*And* we'll figure out how to make the timing work for the jury exhibit."

Mom purses her lips and takes a drink from her glass. "Well, maybe not a schmo off the street."

My pulse pounds in my head. I'm about to argue my case

again, but Dad's ringing phone interrupts. He stands and turns his back to the table. "Yeah?" He puts a hand on his hip. "Are you sure?" Runs his hand through his hair. "I want a thorough search. Keep me posted." When he turns again and looks at me, his face is grave.

8

Danny

I peer through the windshield, my fingers digging into the seat as memories play out like a movie in my head. I'm eleven years old. It's night and we're driving home on the 101. I'm in the backseat, my stomach full of spaghetti and soda, and I'm watching streetlights tick past. Each one flashes a sliver of light across the dashboard, the seats, my legs. The car zooms around the big curve at Pima, pressing me into my seat belt. I can just make out the dark edge of the McDowell Mountains. I touch one finger to the window and block out a star. The road straightens and the streetlights blur. There's a jolt. A bang. A squeal. Then the wall and a heaving crush of metal.

The last time I was in a car with my parents, we crashed. They died.

Dad catches me looking at him in the rearview mirror. I can't take my eyes off him.

A car cuts us off. He pounds the horn. I brace myself against Mom's headrest and double-check that my seat belt's clicked.

"Parker, please." Mom's hand grips the dash, but her voice stays calm. "Take it easy."

"Guy almost clipped us."

"We aren't in a hurry."

He catches a break in the traffic and speeds us over to the far lane, where things are moving. I look out the side window and try to breathe.

"Slow down," Mom says. "I think he's getting carsick."

Dad looks at me again and the car slows. A little. "What were you doing at the mall?" he asks.

"Parker."

"We have a right to know."

Mom points at the dash. Dad shakes his head. "Fine. We'll talk later."

Traffic backs up, then stops altogether. Up ahead, barricades merge all the lanes down to one. "What's going on?" I ask.

"Checkpoint," Dad says.

"For what?"

Mom gives me a look. Dad doesn't answer. We creep along, letting some cars in, keeping others out, until finally it's our turn. Soldiers with semiautomatics slung over their shoulders guard the road. One carries a long-handled mirror. Another holds the leash of a mean-looking dog. A third leans into Dad's window while the other two walk slowly around the car.

"Identification."

Dad hands over his ID. The soldier swipes it through a scanner. "Parker Ogden?"

"Yes."

The guard leans in. "Rebecca Ogden?"

Mom nods.

"Need a verbal reply, ma'am."

"Yes." Mom's voice cracks.

Then it's my turn. "Daniel?"

"Yeah."

"What is your destination, Mr. Ogden?"

"Home."

"Confirm your address."

"Thirty-seven twenty-seven Del Mar."

The soldier gives each of us a once-over. His eyes are hard, like he's seen some bad stuff go down. When he looks at me, I don't flinch. I've seen a lot of bad stuff, too. The guard with the dog passes behind him and says, "All clear."

The soldier hands Dad his ID card and waves us forward with two fingers.

"Out in force," Dad mutters as he rolls his window back up. The car accelerates and he merges back into traffic.

"What did you expect?" Mom turns a little in her seat. "Doing okay back there?"

No, I'm not okay. I'm in a car with my dead parents. They just picked me up from a bombed-out disaster. There are checkpoints guarded by soldiers with guns. I'm in the freaking twilight zone.

The road rises. A blazing orange sunset fills the horizon and glitters across the ocean. I grab Mom's headrest and lean forward. Docked boats bob in a harbor. Farther on, a seawall sticks out into the water. At the end stands a lighthouse. We're in *California*? The freeway turns and I crane my neck to watch the water disappear behind us. High-rises take over the skyline again. Neon signs and flashy billboards advertise Phoenix businesses. Pest control. Boat rentals. Seaside property.

Not California. But definitely not the Phoenix I know.

Dad turns the car onto a street lined with trees and pulls into the driveway of the fourth house on the right. It's blue, with a grassy front yard. A boat sits on a trailer to the side of the garage.

I've never seen the place before. It makes the foster home look even worse than the dump it is. Was? I don't even know.

Dad pulls the key from the ignition and the dome light clicks on. He exhales and lets his head fall forward. Mom reaches over and touches his arm.

His hair is thinner than I remember. His eyes more tired. He pats Mom's hand before going around to help her out.

Mom's even more different than Dad. She uses her cane to push herself out of the seat, her other hand holding on to Dad's. What happened to her? I remember her running alongside me when I learned to ride a bike and dancing with Dad in the kitchen. She was never like this.

I close the car door for her. She taps the necklace around my neck. "Told you it would protect you." We both look at the iridescent square hanging from the leather cord. Her eyes are the same. And her smile. She reaches for my forehead, but she holds back. "Does it hurt?"

"Yeah." I wince, hoping she doesn't touch the bruise.

I watch them walk toward the house. Someone's gonna

jump out of the bushes with a camera and tell me none of this is real, right? That it's all a joke and I'm still a loser orphan in a crummy foster home. *Look how we fooled you. Made you hope. Ha.*

But no one jumps out. There is no camera.

Mom turns on the living room light and goes into the kitchen. Dad walks halfway across the room and stops, his hands on his hips. Along the walls are pictures of the three of us, and some of just me, all of them taken in places I don't recognize, doing things I don't remember. Rafting down a river. Standing like a superhero on top of a tree stump. Chasing birds on a beach. Asleep in the backseat with my head against the window.

It's like a completely different life.

A completely different me.

I put my hand on the wall as the realization hits.

It *is* another me. But how?

"Are you going to tell me what you were doing there?" Dad crosses his arms.

I have no idea what to say. I don't even know where "there" was.

"We thought you were on your way to school," he says. Mom joins him at the doorway. "I think we at least deserve an explanation."

"I . . ." My brain scrambles for something to tell them. All I come up with is, "Everything's kind of a blur."

"It's one thing to hear the emergency announcement. But when the phone rings and they say your son is hurt?" He shakes his head. "You were supposed to be with Germ, going to school. Not at a parade on the other side of town."

Germ? Parade?

"Were you painting?" Mom asks. "Tagging? Or whatever you call it?"

"You promised you'd be careful." Dad runs a hand over his face. "You know every inch of that place had to be covered by Spectrum."

"Spectrum?"

"I know," he says, holding up his hands. "Don't start. But I'm not the one in the hot seat this time. You are. So whenever you're ready to tell us why you lied, we're all ears."

I cross my arms but that doesn't feel right, so I stuff my hands into my pockets. Brent never asks me to explain. He just beats the crap out of me until I swear I'll never do anything ever again. Not even breathe, if that's what he wants. Whatever it takes to make him stop pounding on me. I wish I knew what to say here, but I have no clue why he—I—wasn't at school. I don't know squat. I look again at the kid grinning in the photos. Who is this other me and what am I doing here instead of him?

My parents—*my not-dead parents*—stand there, waiting for something I can't give. It's too much. The walls feel like they're closing in. I don't know what else to do but push past them and run down the hall, away.

Once I find his room, I close the door and fall onto my knees, dizzy. Bury my head in my hands and try to breathe.

This can't be real. It isn't possible. You don't just get sucked through darkness to a different world. That kind of thing only happens in science fiction movies.

When my head stops spinning, I look around. Feel the carpet under my hands. Breathe in the air. It's all real. I don't know how, but it is. I'm really here.

The room is spotless. Even the bed is made. My room at the foster home is piled up with all kinds of crap. This guy, though? Total neat freak.

The walls are covered in posters and art. Crazy stuff, like graffiti you see on the sides of buildings and in alleys. Lots of other things tacked on the walls, too. Police tape. A broken skateboard. There's a nightstand with a lamp and, over by the window, a desk with lined-up books. Art? Poetry? Comics? Well, comics are okay, I guess.

I pick up the MP3 player from the desk, put the earbuds in and press PLAY. Guitars scream, but the song title scrolling across reads *Mozart Piano Concerto No. 10.* I don't know much about classical music, but that's definitely not Mozart. It's decent, though. Kind of like the stuff I listen to. I let it play while I continue to hunt.

There's a pair of shoes under the bed—skater kind—and a notebook with ink and pencil sketches. The top two dresser drawers are full of junk. Probably where he stashes everything when he cleans his room. I find some money in there and shove it into my pocket. The desk is full of pens, folded-up pieces of paper, photos of people I don't know. That leaves the closet, which—surprise—is full of clothes. T-shirts mostly. Sweatshirts. Jeans. Some shorts. More skater shoes and a skateboard. I check the trucks and wheels. It's been a long time since I've ridden, but this'll do if I need to get around. I set it down and look up. Tucked high, almost out of sight, is a duffel bag. I test a lower shelf, then step on it like a ladder. Reaching, I can barely touch the edge of the bag. I stretch higher, grabbing with the tips of my fingers. One of the earbuds falls out, but I keep reaching, wishing my arm would grow longer. My fingers pinch the fabric and I tug the bag toward me, inch by inch, until I get my hand on it and pull. The whole thing comes crashing down. I turn to catch it, then jump back, smacking into the wall behind me. There's a skinny blond guy standing at the door, watching. He takes one look at my face and doubles over.

"Dude," he says, gasping, "that was epic. Your face!" And he laughs so hard he looks like he's gonna pop.

I set the bag down and tell my fists not to punch him.

"Didn't mean to scare you like that, Og." He steps toward me, catching my hand in his and leaning in to clap me on the shoulder. "But you kinda deserved it, you jerk. Scared the crap out of me this morning. When I saw that second one go off, I thought for sure you were toast."

He was there.

I watch him go to the desk, flip the chair around and sit in it backward. Who is this guy? He picks up a Hacky Sack and tosses it from hand to hand. "Sure wasn't the plan they told us, huh? Hey, you going out?" He nods at the bag.

"No, I was just ... checking something." I toss the MP3 player on the bed, crouch down and unzip the bag. It's full of spray paint cans.

"That's a serious knob you got on your head."

I look up. "Huh? Oh. Yeah."

"Does it hurt?"

I search through the bag, looking for who knows what. "Yeah."

"Is that all you can say now? How hard did you smack your melon, anyway?" He looks at my face and stops smiling. "Sorry, dude. I'm just happy to see you, you know? After . . . all that."

I toss the bag back into the closet and sit on the edge of the bed. Looks like I'll have to get answers from this clown. My gut tells me not to bring up how I got here or that I'm a different Danny. Not yet, at least. "All what? It's pretty much a blur for me."

"How much do you remember?"

I shrug. "Nothing?"

"Seriously? Well, it went like this: We got there, we did our thing, and the place went *boom*."

"Didn't you get hurt?"

"My ears keep ringing, but that's it. I was way over on the other side, remember?" He studies my face. "You don't, do you?"

I shake my head.

Two taps on the door and Mom looks in. "Oh, hello, Germ. I didn't realize you were here."

Germ. Dad mentioned him. He catches me looking at him and makes a goofy face. "Hey, Mrs. O."

"I was just checking on Danny," she says, walking over to me. Her left leg seems to be the weaker one. "How's my peanut?"

Germ snorts.

"Don't you start, Jeremy Bulman, or I'll call you nicknames, too." She looks at my forehead. "Doing okay?"

I reach up to touch the bruise but she smacks my hand away. "Leave it alone." She holds my chin and turns my face for a better look. "It'll take a while for that to go down." She smiles at me so long it gets a little awkward. "Okay," she finally says, "you boys be good." And she shuffles from the room, closing the door behind her.

I reach up to search out the most painful parts on my forehead. Germ imitates Mom. "Don't go touching your owies, Peanut."

"Feels like it's crawling with ants."

"Here." Germ walks over. "You scratch and I'll tell you if you're getting close or not."

Good plan. It works. A couple of well-placed scratches later, the ants have stopped crawling, except at the center of the goose egg, but that part doesn't itch so much as throb.

"Can you believe school's gonna be open on Monday? Sucks." He kicks the Hacky off his shoe. It falls to the floor and he tries again. "But hey, all the girls are gonna swoon when they hear you were hurt. God, I can just see Angela Sweeney now." He holds the Hacky Sack up like a head and his voice goes high. "Ooh, Danny, let me make it all better." He gives it the grossest pretend kiss ever. I laugh even as I wonder who the heck Angela Sweeney is.

"Seriously, Og-dog. Girls are gonna lie down at your feet. You should milk this for all it's worth."

"Whatever." I shake my head. I don't know about this Danny, but girls have never dug me.

He kicks the Hacky Sack. "So what do we tell them?"

"About what?"

He gets to ten and it lands two feet away. "About this morning." He motions for me to stand. It's been forever since I tried Hacky. He does three kicks off his right foot and passes it to me. I do two and it flops to the carpet.

"I don't think we should tell anyone anything." I scoop it back up and launch it to him. He gets to twelve before it falls.

"People will ask why we were there." He lobs it back to me and I kick it. Maybe I can match his ten.

"My parents did." Five. Six. "I didn't know what to tell them." Seven.

"You didn't mention RD, did you?"

Eight, and it drops. "What's RD?" I grab the Hacky with my heels and kick it up.

Germ catches it on his knee and starts his own count. His face is scrunched with concentration or anger, I can't tell which. "You don't remember *Red December*?"

"I . . ." God, this is hard.

"Dude." He tosses the Hacky to me and I catch it with my left foot. Lob to the right. One. Two. Three. "Anarchist group?"

Four. Five.

"Wants to overthrow the government?"

Six. Seven. Eight.

"This morning was our last job with them?"

My feet stop kicking. The Hacky drops to the floor.

9

EEVEE

I'm putting the final touches on my press conference updo when Dad knocks twice and leans against the doorjamb of my room. Mom steps out from behind him. "Got a second, honey?"

Uh-oh.

"Sure." I push another bobby pin into place to buy some time, then follow them down the hall to the family room. Mom sits uncomfortably close to me on the couch. "What's up?" I ask. "Something wrong?"

Dad's tie hangs loose, like he always keeps it before he's about to make a big speech. "Eve . . ." He clears his throat and makes his serious politician face. "There was a . . . um . . . development in matters related to yesterday's attack."

I look at Mom. She reaches over and takes my hands. "What is it?"

"The second device detonated near ShopMart, south of the mall. The building caught fire and it spread unchecked through the stores nearby." He looks me in the eye. "Including Jansen Fine Arts Services."

"Wait. What?" I pull my hands free and stand. My heart feels like it's trying to break out of my chest. Mom stands, too, and puts her arm around me but I shrug her away and grab the back of the chair.

"The fire has been put out," Dad says. "And I've given the crews explicit orders to locate what's left of your paintings, but . . ." He makes his condolence face.

"What's left?" My mind reels. The room telescopes, tilts. I feel like I'm standing outside myself, watching my life unravel. "Maybe there was a mistake."

"I'm afraid not, honey," he says. "We were going to wait to tell you, but we decided you had a right to know."

Take it back, I want to scream. *Take back what you said. Take this all away.* But instead, I wander over to the window and stare out beyond my reflection. Tears blur the city into circles of white and gold. This can't be happening. Not to me. Not now. I touch the window, press against it, wishing I could push right through. Mom puts her hand on my shoulder. "I'm sorry, Eve."

"No, you're not." I swat her hand away. "You're happy this happened, aren't you? This is the best news ever, isn't it?"

Her face changes from shock to anger. "Of course not! How could you say that?"

"Because now I can't apply for the internship!" I wipe away tears. "Now I get to stay home, just like you want!"

"Eve." Dad's voice is firm. "Apologize now."

"This isn't my fault," Mom says. "It's just an unfortunate—"

I don't let her finish. I run back to the safety of my room

and slam the door. Even with it shut, I hear them yelling. At me. At each other. I throw myself on the bed and drown out the world with a pillow.

Those paintings were my ticket out, to somewhere I can be myself. I can't stay here. Defiance kicks up inside, daring me to lash out, to do something reckless. It's the same feeling that got me in trouble the night Vivian caught me in the vaults. I try to stifle it by pounding my fists into the bed. I'm about to pound the wall when there's a knock at the door. "Eve." It's Dad again.

"Go away."

"I know you're upset," he says. "But we're going to get through this. We just need to stick together."

My world's crumbling, and he's spouting lines from political speeches? There comes another knock, so loud it startles me. "We're leaving in an hour," Mom yells. "You better be ready." Her footsteps pound back down the hallway and everything goes quiet, but I can tell Dad is still standing out there. I throw the pillow aside, walk over and open the door.

His head tilts to the right and he puts his hand on my shoulder. For a split second I see the real him. Not the governor. My dad. But as quickly as it came, it's gone and I'm face to face again with the politician. "Try to get yourself together, okay? We need to put on a brave face for the public."

Gray clouds hang low in the sky as Jonas drives us north toward the outskirts of the city, away from the Tower complex and high-rise buildings downtown. Dad talks to Richard on his phone, fine-tuning his speech, while Mom fusses with her nails. Both of them pretend there isn't a ticking bomb sitting between them. My eyes are dried out from crying and my nose is red despite the makeup. On the outside, I've pulled myself together the best I can. Inside, I'm a mess.

The city whooshes by outside the window. When the freeway swings around toward the coast, white smoke from what used to be the mall rises into view. I avert my eyes and fight back tears. I had to redo my makeup once already. Mom pulls a mirror from her purse and checks her reflection. Dad tells Richard to give legislators a heads-up; he's going to call a special session and, no, he doesn't care what Senator Hayes thinks.

Vivian's words rush at me. *I'm applying to Belford.* My heart races. I grip my chest, suddenly feeling like I can't breathe.

With my paintings gone, I won't get into Belford. But she still might.

Mom holds out her lip gloss. I stare at it, but all I see is Vivian's smiling face. She'll never let me live it down. Mom gives the gloss a little shake and says, "Cameras." Rather than start another fight, I take it and dab it on my lips. Dad hangs up the phone and practices saying *solemn occasion* over and over.

I imagine myself made of paper, a hollowed-out shell. Instead of lip gloss, I hold a match. Starting from my lips, a line of flame consumes me. For a moment I hold my shape, then fall into a pile of soot on the car seat. Dad whispers, "Solemn occasion." Mom rolls down the window. The rush of air scatters me across the road.

10

DANNY

Dad checks twice before pulling wide into traffic. The truck engine groans under the heavy load. Once we're in the lane, we both look out the cab window to make sure the boat made it, too.

He woke me super early. Knocked on the door and said, "It's time." Kinda scared me. Time for what? I stumbled out of bed, groggy and sore from yesterday. Threw on some clothes and found my way to the kitchen. He was standing at the counter with a coffee mug in his hand. Took one look at me and said, "You're wearing that?"

I looked down at what I'd put on. Camo shorts and a long-sleeved T-shirt with the neck ripped out.

"It's cold out on the water."

That's when I remembered the ocean, and the boat parked next to the garage. This wasn't scary. It was awesome. I ran back down the hall, changed into jeans and pulled a flannel over the shirt. Grabbed shoes and socks from the closet and raced back to the kitchen, but he wasn't there. I finally found him out front, checking the hitch on the trailer. "That's more like it," he said. "Climb in."

I can count the number of times I've seen the ocean on one finger. Now I'm going out on an actual boat. That sound? That'd be my mind blowing. I look at him, the stubble on his chin, the way he rests his wrist on top of the steering wheel, and a feeling of peace floods over me. I'm sitting next to my *dad*. This is how it should be. This is how my life was supposed to be.

"Danny," he says, shifting into third. He doesn't take his eyes off the road. Old-time rockabilly hovers just above the engine noise. I try to identify the songs, struggling to latch onto words and guitar licks, but the volume is too low. "I'm sorry for coming down so hard on you yesterday. But you can't just leave us hanging. You need to tell us what's going on."

And like that, the good feeling's gone. For a second I think, *Tell him.* Tell him you're not their son. Tell him you're a different Danny from a different world. I even open my mouth to speak but can't get myself to say it. He'll think I'm crazy. How do I tell him that, in my Phoenix, he and Mom are dead? Besides, I don't want to ruin this. Even if I don't understand what's going on or how I got here, sitting in this truck talking to him makes all the crap I've been through worth it.

"This lack of communication," he says, shaking his head, "it's not okay." He shifts into fourth and returns his hand to the wheel. "Your mom and I deserve better than that, don't you think?"

All I can do is nod.

"Listen, I know things have been pretty intense lately. I

haven't been around as much because of work and . . . well, all kinds of stuff. But that doesn't give me an excuse to take it out on you. I'm sorry."

Whoa. He thinks that was being hard on me? He has no idea. As I watch him driving, I realize how much I don't know—but *want* to know—about him. "What's going on at work?" I don't even know what he does for a living.

"Oh, you know, the usual. They want everything done last week but there's more work than the team can—" He stops midsentence and reaches for the stereo knob. "Hang on."

A man's voice has replaced the music. Dad turns it up a notch and his hands go tight again around the wheel.

". . . a tracking and detection technology known as Skylar. Both efficient and effective, Skylar will provide a blanket of security for our city and take us one step closer to being able to sleep soundly at night, knowing there is an ever-watching eye—"

"Who is that?" I ask.

"Governor."

"Soon we will provide you—first the citizens of Phoenix, then all the communities of Arizona—with the opportunity to be part of the solution as well."

Dad's face sours. "Son of a—" He jabs the stereo power button, leaving only the sound of the truck engine around us.

"What did he mean, 'be part of the solution'?"

"It means we don't have much time."

"Until what?"

"Until they've got us all completely clamped down." He glares at the radio. "You hear that? Did you hear what I said?!"

He's like a crazy person.

"Listen to me, son," he says, holding up a finger. "No more taking risks. Keep your head down. Don't give them any reason to suspect you. Promise?"

I remember what Germ said about that anarchist group we're involved with, and the job we did with them.

"Promise."

"Good." He says it a few more times under his breath, like he's trying to convince himself.

We drive on in silence. I can tell he's chewing on what the governor said. I wish I knew what it all meant.

Dad looks in his side mirror and across into mine. "What now?" He brakes and pulls over to the curb. "Stay quiet." I can't see around the boat, but that kind of talk can only mean one thing.

A cop knocks on the glass. Dad rolls down the window and hands over his license.

"Heading for the harbor?" The cop taps a device on his wrist, then scans Dad's ID.

"Nice day," Dad says. "Thought we'd take the boat out."

"Aren't you aware the harbor is restricted at this time?"

Dad sighs. "No, sir. I wasn't aware—"

"Do you pay attention to the security broadcast announcements?"

"Yes."

"Then you'd know the harbor is closed, Mr. . . ." He checks the screen on his wrist. "Ogden."

"I must have missed it."

The cop looks across the cab at me. "Are you Daniel?"

"Yes."

The cop looks back at Dad, holds his gaze for a long time and says, "Mind if I look at your rig?"

"No, sir. Do I need to get out?"

"Stay in the vehicle, please."

I watch the cop check out the truck and boat. Dad claps his hand on my knee. "Relax. It's okay."

The cop walks by my window, kicks the tire and continues around the front to Dad's side. "Tires look a bit worn. Best have them looked at."

"Will do."

"No point going to the harbor. They'll turn you back around."

"Understood."

The cop reads and taps his wrist screen again. Finally, he nods. "Pay attention to the security bulletins."

"Yes, sir." Dad waits for him to drive off before starting up the truck and moving back into traffic. "Looks like we'll have to try another day." He shifts gears and says, "Sorry," like it's his fault.

I can't help but wonder if it's mine.

11

EEVEE

Forty minutes later, Jonas exits the freeway and we drive past outlet malls and subdivisions to the foothills of the McDowell Mountains. I've only been to DART one other time, when Dad cut the ribbon to open a new research wing years ago. I don't remember it looking like this. At the main parking area, Jonas swings a left, passing a large metal sign dominated by a fingerprint logo. The lot is packed with media vehicles. Trees and bushes grow thick along the road, blocking the low-lying building from view. Finally, we wind around a circular drive, where reporters and camera crews wait, ready with questions for the governor. Richard approaches the car wearing his usual anxious expression. Jonas opens the door, letting Dad out first.

Mom hesitates and turns back toward me. "Despite what you think, I am sorry about your paintings," she says in a low voice. Then she gets out of the car and I follow.

As soon as Dad steps onto the curb, the reporters start in. Richard holds up his hands. "Governor Solomon will read a statement before taking questions." He sees Dad to the podium. Mom and I stand a little off to his side. I check my reflection in the building's glass front. My eyes are puffy. I quickly straighten my skirt.

Richard leans in and whispers something to Dad. He nods and pulls a paper from his coat pocket.

"Thank you for being here on this solemn occasion. Will you please join me in a moment of silence out of respect for those affected by Friday's events?"

The crowd shifts and quiets. I fold my hands and lower my head. Feet shuffle on the concrete. A breeze blows through the entryway. A man clears his throat.

"Thank you," Dad finally says, and the microphones move back around him. He holds the podium with both hands. "On Friday, Phoenix suffered a terrible attack on the Patriot Day parade, an attack perpetrated by the cowards known as Red December. We meet here today at the Department of Advanced Research Technologies not only to discuss safety measures currently in place to protect our citizens but to unveil a new solution in detecting and preventing the growing threats against our society.

"It is with pride and humility," he says, smoothing a hand down his tie, "that I announce Phoenix has been chosen for the beta testing of a tracking and detection technology known as Skylar. Both efficient and effective, Skylar will provide a blanket of security for our city and take us one step closer to being able to sleep soundly at night, knowing there is an ever-watching eye looking over us. With your participation, we can make this happen.

"After this press conference, my family"—he looks at us, and all the reporters do, too. Mom nudges me in the back to stand straighter—"and I will voluntarily register with Skylar and will therefore officially be part of the solution. Soon we will provide you—first the citizens of Phoenix, then all the communities of Arizona—with the opportunity to be part of the solution as well. It is easy. It is painless. And it will mean the difference between vulnerability and security." He holds one hand up to emphasize the big finish. "Only by working together do we ensure the promise of our future. As always, my thoughts and the thoughts of my wife and daughter are with the families of the victims. Thank you."

Flawless execution.

The press jumps in again with questions.

"Is it true you've called a special legislative session?"

Surprise flashes across Dad's face. "Yes."

"Can you elaborate on how Skylar works?"

"Preapproved members of the media will follow us into the DART facility, where the system will be explained. Photos and video will be released to the public."

"Was there any warning before the attack?"

"No."

"How long will the rolling blackouts continue?"

"I'm assured the system will stabilize soon."

"How do you respond to critics who say Friday's attack is just another sign of the failure of your administration?"

"I'd say those critics should spend less time whining and more time working toward the betterment of society." Dad holds up his hands. "That's all for now. Thank you."

Dad guides Mom and me toward the door Richard holds open for us. As we pass, Dad mutters, "Find out who at the legislature is talking, and end it. And next time only allow in reporters who adhere to approved questions."

"Yes, sir." Richard leaves us in the lobby.

Mom brushes the shoulder of Dad's suit jacket. "Nicely done."

He winks at her, but his face remains stern until Richard returns, followed by a reporter and a photographer. Dad smiles and extends his hand to welcome them.

"Smile," Mom says under her breath.

"I don't feel like smiling."

"That doesn't matter," she whispers with her jaw clenched. "Smile anyway."

I stretch my mouth into a grimace.

"You can do better than that. Think of something happy."

Happy? Nothing could make me happy right now.

●

We move from the lobby's polished concrete floors to a large conference room. Several DART employees in lab coats stand along the far wall. A few more sit with their backs to us, facing laptops. The screens in the room display spooling lines of code and what look like GPS coordinates. The main screen at the front shows the framework of a building with yellow dots meandering inside. Now and again a pop-up window displays the name and coordinates of a particular dot.

A woman with dark hair welcomes us as the press photographer snaps pictures. "Please remember," she says, "for security reasons, you may not photograph any of the information displayed on the screens." Turning to us again, she says, "Good afternoon, Governor. Mrs. Solomon. Miss Solomon. I'm Dr. Anna Owens, director of research. These are the members of the Skylar engineering team, led by Dr. Marcus McAllister."

A tall man with a beard and glasses steps forward to shake our hands. "Welcome to DART," he says. "Or as we like to call it, the central nervous system." Dad chuckles and a couple of onlookers join in. Dr. McAllister motions to the screens. "What you're looking at is Skylar, a comprehensive framework that will provide unprecedented monitoring capabilities and protection for the citizens of large metropolitan areas. This is a graphic representation of the DART facility. The yellow dots represent every individual in the building." He places a hand on the shoulder of an employee seated in front of a laptop. When the guy turns, I realize it's Warren, my study partner. I knew he interned at DART, but I didn't realize he worked on stuff like *this*. I give him a small wave, but he doesn't notice.

"Warren," Dr. McAllister says, "will you go close on 132, please?"

Warren's fingers race over the keyboard, and the screen zooms in on a room containing yellow dots and red Xs. Dr. McAllister walks out the door, and one of the dots leaves the room. When the dot returns, so does the doctor.

"So that's a representation of this room?" Dad asks.

"Very good, Governor." Dr. McAllister shuts the door.

"And the red Xs?"

Dr. McAllister nods at Warren and the view zeroes in. "The red Xs are Unknowns, individual signals located by but unidentifiable in the Skylar system." He waves another assistant over, a woman with dark hair and cat-eye glasses who's not much older than me. She rolls a small machine toward us and detaches a handheld unit. Stitched on her lab coat is the name NINA.

"Hold still, please." She presses a button on the unit and moves the pen-shaped wand over Dad's head, starting at his left shoulder, moving to his right, and back again to the left. The photographer snaps photos. Another press of the button and Dad's red X blips to a yellow dot.

"Abracadabra," Dr. McAllister says at the same time Dad says, "Fascinating."

Nina follows the same procedure with Mom, who smiles extra wide for the camera.

Nina turns toward me and I step back. She frowns.

"Eve," Mom warns, her voice saccharine.

"What does it do?" I ask, pointing at the screen. "How did it do that?"

Nina looks at Dr. McAllister like she needs his permission to speak. He nods. "It reads your EMF signature," she says.

"My what?"

Nina withdraws her arm and gives me a patient smile. Dr. Owens moves in. "Every human emits an electromagnetic field. Our research found that each EMF carries a signature unique to the body emitting it. The system logs the reading of the EMF, linking it to a sister database of the Spectrum system already in place. Our building houses a grid network that utilizes scalar waves to track EMFs, isolating positions and movements according to GPS coordinates. It's quite simple, really."

"It doesn't hurt." Dad holds up a hand to stop the photographer from taking pictures.

"Honey." Mom's voice is losing its sweetness. "Don't make them wait."

"Will people have a choice whether or not to be in the system?" I ask. Warren turns in his seat to look at me. The reporter scribbles notes. "I mean, people won't be forced into this, will they?"

"Of course not," Dr. Owens says with a laugh. "It's completely voluntary, just like Spectrum. Once people see the benefits—no more missing children, no more dementia patients walking away from facilities and getting lost, not to mention overall increased security—they'll ask to be added."

"Who doesn't want increased security, right?" Dad says. "Especially after Friday."

"Exactly," Dr. McAllister says. "Criminals, of course, are a different matter. They'll be automatically scanned upon apprehension."

"What do you say, Miss Solomon?" Dr. Owens steps toward me. "Let's change that Unknown to a Known."

I eye the wand in Nina's hand. "Okay."

"Hold still, please." Nina moves the wand over my head. I don't feel anything. She presses a button and another red X blips to a yellow dot. I'm no longer Unknown, and I'm not quite sure how I feel about it.

"There," Dr. Owens says as Nina wheels the equipment away. "Simple, isn't it?"

"Warren," Dr. McAllister says, "switch to the virtual grid view."

Warren turns back in his seat and types. The large screen switches to a graphic representation of Phoenix littered with dots and Xs. "This is an offline representation of the network established over Phoenix. You can see we still need to expand to cover some of the outlying sectors. We should have those connection points established early next week, and Skylar will be ready to go live the week after."

"But you've tested the system, correct?" Dad asks.

"Oh yes," Dr. Owens says. "We've run several tests—the most recent on Friday morning. All of them have been successful."

"Perfect." Dad nods his approval. "How soon before we begin public rollout?"

"Mobile sign-ups begin next week," Dr. McAllister says.

"Right on schedule." Dad smiles at the reporter. "Just how I like it."

"How about a group photo?" the photographer asks. I follow Mom and Dad to stand beside Dr. Owens and Dr. McAllister.

"Smile," Mom says just before the camera flashes.

Something brushes my hand and I turn. Warren faces the laptop, fingers typing away. I start to say something to him, but he gives a quick shake of his head. My eye catches the yellow dot—me—on the big screen. I bury my hand, and the note he tucked into it, in my suit pocket and follow the others out of the room. Mom waits for me by the door. When I get close enough, she puts her hand at the back of my neck and hisses in my ear, "How dare you embarrass your father like that."

12

DANNY

Dad doesn't go straight home. Instead, he makes a wide turn, pulling into a grocery store parking lot. The sign says ABBOT'S in big red letters. "Let's surprise Mom with lunch." He parks out where the lot is empty, taking up two spots because of the boat. I hop out and close the door, scaring away a couple of seagulls picking at a hamburger wrapper.

We walk together toward the entrance. Dad claps me on the back. "I'm thinking pizza. How about you?"

"Sounds good." The doors slide open and I follow him inside, thanking my lucky stars I didn't wake up in a world without pizza.

The store is pretty much the same as the ones back home. We walk past piles of fruit in the produce section. Vases of flowers in a fridge. Aisles of bread and cereal boxes. Signs announcing specials and prices hanging from the ceiling. I follow Dad toward one that says CAFÉ. The lights flicker. Dad bumps me on the arm. "Grab some milk, would ya?"

"Oh. Uh . . ." I look around. "Sure."

I turn into the pet food aisle, wondering which way to go. When I reach the end, I make a left, looking for signs. Farther down is a refrigerated case of cheese. I follow it to butter, sour cream, orange juice and, finally, milk.

What kind do they drink? There's a gazillion to choose from. I try to find one that looks like what we drank at the foster home. It had a blue cap.

A girl walks up from behind me and opens the refrigerator case. Her hair falls in waves down her back, and she's wearing flip-flops with her business suit. She hesitates before picking containers from the yogurt section, stacking them on top of each other in the crook of her arm. One slips and she tries to catch it but only manages to keep the others from falling, too.

"Here," I say, reaching down to pick it up.

"Thanks." She balances the containers in her left arm while using her right to pull her hair back from her face.

She's beautiful. Dark hair and eyes. There's something familiar about her. For a second I forget what I'm doing, why I'm standing in the dairy section holding a container of lemon-raspberry yogurt.

Then her eyes meet mine and she steps back, surprised. "It's you." Her voice is soft, barely a whisper.

Me? I look down at myself as if expecting to see someone else.

The lights flicker. When they go out, she makes a small *oh* sound. Even though it's daytime, our corner at the back of the store goes dark. She takes a step toward me. As my eyes adjust, I can make out her hair and shoulders. Her hand grasps my arm.

A voice calls, "Miss Solomon?"

She inhales like she's going to say something, but instead she lets go and moves away into the dark.

"Wait." I take two steps and run into a display. Boxes fall, banging loudly against the floor. Awesome. Way to make an impression, Ogden.

The lights in the refrigerator case blink on, chasing shadows from the place where we stood. I look for her, but she's gone. Who was she? She acted like she knew me. A voice comes over the store PA system. "Attention, Abbot's shoppers. We apologize . . ." I walk back to the dairy section, pick up the mess I made and try to remember what I'd been doing there in the first place.

"Well, that was annoying." Dad walks up, holding a pizza box. "What's the matter? Couldn't find the milk? It's right here." He grabs a half gallon from the case. "Come on. Let's go pay for this stuff."

My eyes search the aisles as we walk to the front of the store. It's like she's just disappeared. By the time we leave, I'm almost convinced I imagined the whole thing.

13

EEVEE

Sunday morning, the reality of the last forty-eight hours rushes at me, bringing with it a sense of dread. Images flash through my mind: a shopping mall in ruins; reporters gathered; Dad at my bedroom door; Mom's whisper in my ear; a column of white smoke; a red *X* amid yellow dots; his face just before the lights went out.

Friday morning, Vivian Hayes was the worst of my problems. Now look at the world.

I roll onto my back to see the stars swirl above. My eyes follow the blue and yellow brushstrokes making their way toward the orange moon shining over a sleepy village. My breathing slows. My hands stop strangling the sheets.

I reach under my mattress and pull out the Retrogressives book. Someday I'll return it to the Archives. But not today. My fingers flip through the pages, pausing on Klee's *Dance of a Melancholic Child II* to trace the girl's delicate fingers and heart-shaped lips. Her teardrop eye and umbrella nose. I hold the book close, studying how the colors blend behind her, creating a kind of red halo. Looking across the room at my own version on the easel, I see how much I still have to learn.

My fingers continue their journey, passing Picasso's *Old Guitarist,* Chagall's *Between Darkness and Light.* Another Klee, *Blossoms in the Night.* Van Gogh's *At Eternity's Gate.* The last page is where my fingers stop, on Ramsey's *Iterations.*

I can't believe I saw him again, and in a grocery store, of all places. So strange. I run my hand over the smooth photo, remembering the feel of the real thing, remembering the night of Bosca's exhibit.

I was angry after he demoted me. But not just at Bosca. At Vivian, too. And at the ones who decide what is and isn't good, who watch everything we say and do and tell us to rat out those who think or act outside the norm.

It's like there are two sides of me. The good girl—the governor's daughter, the face of polite society—and the other girl, the one who steals books of banned art and finds beauty in what others consider ugly and unfit.

I walked the museum's back hallways that night, feeling the two sides wrestling for control. When I came across a service door leading outside, I propped it open with one of my shoes—last thing I needed was to get locked out—then leaned back against the wall and closed my eyes. The city hummed around me. People meandered toward the museum entrance. Traffic streamed by on Central. The light-rail whooshed along its tracks.

When I opened my eyes, I saw him standing there, watching me.

"You're not supposed to be here," I said.

He shrugged, like the rules didn't apply to him.

I walked across the loading dock, the asphalt rough beneath my feet. Half of his face was in shadow. As I moved closer, a feeling came over me. I felt intrigued. Inspired.

Alive.

He was a total stranger, but I didn't care. All that mattered was that I take that moment and make it my own. My rules. My decision.

So I kissed him.

And then I walked away.

"Hang on," he said. I thought he'd run over to me, maybe, or want my name. Instead, he simply asked, "Why?"

I shrugged, just like he had. Maybe the rules didn't apply to me either. Then I walked through the door, leaving him outside.

I got about five feet and stopped.

Looked back.

One last hurrah for bad Eevee: I propped the door open just long enough for him to grab hold, then I hurried off to be the good girl again.

I saw him a couple of times during the show, but I didn't say anything. I was already in trouble—big trouble—and didn't need to add more to it. It was just a kiss. A moment. Just me taking a stand, even if only to prove something to myself. What? That I'm brave? That I'll be okay?

I fall back on my bed and look up at *Starry Night.* The thing is, I wasn't supposed to see him again. But here I am in trouble, and I run into him at Abbot's. It's like the universe thought I needed a reminder or something.

My phone on the nightstand dings. It's Dad.

Gallery paintings delivered to school. See Bosca.

I tuck the book back under my mattress, then flip all the banned paintings on my walls and ceiling over to their safe sides. A quick trade of jammies for a skirt and tank top and I head out. Time to see how bad the damage is.

14

Danny

Monday morning, Germ drives as far as the park-and-ride, where we swap his car for the light-rail. Everything has me on edge. The unfamiliar neighborhoods, getting checked for explosives before boarding the train, the nervous passengers wary of another attack, having no idea what to expect when we get to school. It's only been three days, but it feels like forever since I walked out of the foster home, went to school and then . . . what? Jumped here? Fell? I replay it over and over in my mind, but I'm nowhere closer to understanding how it happened. Or why. It's like something out of *Star Trek* or something. I even started reading Danny's comic books, hoping to find some kind of clue.

What if I never figure it out? What if I stay here forever, impersonating this other me? Wouldn't be so bad, I guess. His life sure beats the hell out of mine. Parents. Best friend. Girls.

My hand grips the overhead handle tight. I watch buildings and traffic stream by while Germ gives the play-by-play of his weekend. The muscles in my arm flex and relax, tendons bulge and disappear, reacting to the movement of the train. There's a small scar, faded white from time, on the inside of my elbow. I wonder what it's from. This body is so different. Stronger, healthier. And then I realize—

"I haven't craved a smoke since I got here."

"What?"

"Nothing."

He smirks. "Since when do you smoke?"

"I don't."

"Then why'd you say that?"

"Just . . . never mind."

He shakes his head. "Did you know my dad used to smoke? Back when it was legal. Sometimes I catch him holding a pen like a cigarette."

"That's funny." I kinda laugh, but I'm thinking about the other Danny, wondering if he's suddenly craving a cigarette. Wait—smoking is illegal here?

"You okay, man?"

The train rounds a corner and everyone on board shifts. "Sometimes it just feels like I'm on the wrong planet."

"I hear ya." He nods. "This place is getting crazier by the day. Hey, did you guys take the boat out?"

"How did you know?"

"I stopped by and saw it gone."

"Yeah, but we didn't get far. A cop pulled us over and told us the harbor was closed."

"Figures."

The train slows. Germ grabs his backpack, so I do the same.

When the doors open, I follow him onto the platform. Across the busy street stands a huge concrete building fenced in behind tall gates. Students wait in a security line before going through. The sign reads ARCADIA TECH.

That's a high school? Looks more like a prison.

"My dad was going on about that new Skylar thing last night." Germ looks to the right before crossing the street. "He's getting fed up, too, which is saying a lot." When we get closer to the gate, he mutters, "Wish there was something we could do."

I'm not really sure what he's going on about, so I don't say anything.

The line leads to a metal detector. It's like we can't go anywhere without having to pass through some kind of checkpoint. Makes me jumpy. I scan the faces of the other students. Some of them look nervous. The word *Friday* floats around their conversations. The guy in front of me steps through the detector and gets a green light. I set my backpack on the table, walk through and get the green light, too.

The guard unzips my bag and looks through the contents. Even though there's nothing illegal in it—that I know of, anyway—my hands are twitchy. I shove them in my pockets and wait. Inside the gates is a concrete courtyard with huge trees and a few benches. But the students don't hang around like they do back at Palo Brea. As soon as they're through security, they walk up the steps into the building. I count the rows of windows. Five stories tall. Can't see how deep it goes.

"Hey, Ogden." A guy with curly hair waves as he walks by. I nod. No idea who he is. Hanging out in my room is one thing.

Trying to fit in here is going to be impossible. I don't know where to go, who I'm supposed to know—nothing.

Germ bumps me with his elbow. At least I can take cues from him.

We only get about ten feet in when a girl with blond hair steps in my way. "Hi, Danny."

"Hey, uh . . ." I try to act cool. "How ya doin'?"

She flips her hair over her shoulder, leans toward me and, lowering her voice, says, "I heard you were almost killed in the terrorist attack."

Germ holds both hands out at her like, *See?*

"Killed? Nah. Just smacked my head."

"I was there, too," Germ says. "My ears are still ringing."

She raises an eyebrow at him, then turns back to me. "Is it serious?" She stands on her toes to take a closer look at my bruise. "Maybe I could kiss it and make it better."

Um, yes, please?

"We gotta get to class." Germ tugs on my sleeve so hard I lose my balance. "See ya, Angela."

That's Angela?

As Germ pulls me away, I manage to sputter out, "See ya." In no time she's flirting with another guy. He mutters, "What'd I tell you? You get all the"—his voice goes high and girlie—"*Oh, Danny.*" He rolls his eyes. "And I get nothing."

Where I live—or used to live, I guess—it's hot, it never rains and never, *ever* snows, and some people put green rocks in their yards because it's too hard to get grass to grow. And Palo Brea, the school I go to—or *used* to go to—is a bunch of separate buildings that look like airplane hangars connected by sidewalks. To get to your locker, you have to walk halfway across campus. When it's hot out, that totally sucks, which is why I don't bother with books. If I go to school at all.

We don't have metal detectors. We don't have security guards. And we definitely don't have this many people. Geez, it's like swimming upstream. We elbow our way up the stairs to the third floor and I follow Germ into a classroom. It's crammed full of desks. The walls are covered in posters of pillars inscribed with red, white and blue text. Germ grabs a seat near the back and pulls a book from his backpack. Civics. Sounds like a real snoozefest. I take the chair next to him and look in Danny's bag. No book. I almost laugh out loud. Maybe we're not so different after all.

A bald man in a polyester suit walks in and goes right to the whiteboard. "Take a seat. We have a lot to cover today." He uncaps a pen and starts writing: GOVERNMENT. FAMILY. BUSINESS. MEDIA. EDUCATION. RELIGION. ARTS. They're the same as the labels on the pillar posters. "Hurry," he says, watching students fill up the desks. "We don't have all day." The bell rings, and he motions for a girl to close the door. "Due to Friday's events," he says, his right eye twitching, "we'll be postponing our discussion of the Twenty-Ninth Amendment to cover, *again,* the essential components of a functional society."

The class groans.

He launches into a lecture about the government and

people working together to strengthen the course of . . . I don't know. Maybe it's habit or a kink in my brain, but I immediately tune him out. My eyes stare at the board. He writes his *Es* with weird extra loops. My eyelids start to slow-blink, so I shift in my seat, trying to stay awake and learn something about this world.

Then I see her, and suddenly my brain kicks into overdrive.

Sitting two rows over, she's scribbling something in a notebook. She has the same long dark hair as the girl at the grocery store. Is it really her? I lean to the left to get a better look, but her hair is in the way. Lean to the right, but I'm blocked by a guy with big shoulders.

". . . because for everyone to live in peace and security," the teacher says, circling the word RELIGION, "we must adhere to the standards set by our elected leaders.

"Now, when it comes to the next pillar, we see how proper aesthetics in the arts reinforce the ideal . . ."

I scoot my desk for a better view. It scrapes across the floor, making a sound like a sick cat. The teacher looks annoyed, but I don't care. She turns toward the sound and her hair falls away from her face. I hold my breath, but—

Not her.

Not even close.

15

EEVEE

Antonio overturns the last box of scraps onto the worktable and spreads out the pieces. Seeing the tattered remains of what used to be my paintings is overwhelming, but I'm determined not to cry. Whenever my throat feels tight and my eyes begin to burn, I ask myself what daring Eevee would do. The truth is, I don't actually know, but I'm guessing tears wouldn't be an option. So I take a breath and keep going, even though this feels hopeless. When it gets to be too much again, I sigh and press the heels of my hands into my eyes.

"Sigh, yes," he says. "But also work." Resolved to salvage what we can, he chooses another scrap and turns it like a puzzle piece, seeing if it fits with the one next to it. He grunts. It doesn't.

The studio always feels cold, with its cinder block walls and high windows. Even more so today. The smells of linseed oil and turpentine hang in the air. On the table by the door, a small radio pipes out tinny opera arias, his favorite. He hums quietly.

"I think that part went over here." I pick up the same piece, brushing some dirt away, and move it over to my side, where the pieces of the lower half of the painting are supposed to be.

"You think that goes there?" He scowls. "No. That was at the top. Up here." He pokes a fat finger against the wooden tabletop.

"I know my own painting."

He throws up his hands. "And me? I know nothing?" His Calabrian accent grows thick. "I'm only the teacher. I only learn you everything I know so you can be success, but no"—he walks away, shaking his head—"you know more than the teacher."

I push my hair back from my forehead and swallow. The lump in my throat forms again, and I press my hands against the table and breathe until it's gone. Then I grab another piece of mangled canvas from the pile and smooth it out before picking it up to take a closer look. I can't tell if the black is paint or soot. A quick rub of my thumb over a section solves the mystery. Soot. The piece falls as I put my face in my hands. "This is impossible."

"Work!" Antonio calls from across the room, where he stands at his easel, a paint-smudged apron covering his stomach. "Find your way through." He dabs crimson on the chipboard and swirls it with his typical flair. Antonio Bosca, the master.

"Find my way through," I mutter, turning the damaged piece to place it among the wreckage. "Find my way through."

"Yes, *compagna*. Find your way."

He's using his pet name for me. Maybe I'm back in his good graces.

I uncrumple the next piece and my heart leaps into my throat. In my hands is a scrap of *Confidante,* the best painting in my collection. The one I was sure would secure my spot at Belford. I close my eyes and see it whole again in my mind. The long branch adorned in gold leaves and the two birds sitting like shadows, side by side. When I painted it, I worried it was too simple, but Bosca declared my palette-knife technique perfect. The scrap in my hand is of the birds . . . almost. Half of one is torn away. Maybe the rest of it's here somewhere in the pile. Maybe I can find all of the pieces and restore it somehow.

The studio door opens with its familiar squeak and Vivian walks in, chirping a cheery hello. Antonio sets down his brush and greets her with his Continental kiss-kiss.

"Hello, Eevee." She strolls over toward the worktable.

I don't look up. Can't. My hands continue to work through the pieces, my mind clinging to a glimpse of hope. I'm afraid if I stop searching, I'll never get started again.

"What's all this? New project?" She stops on the other side of the table. I keep my head down and scrape dirt away from one of the pieces. "Isn't that . . . ?" She picks up part of my canvas puzzle. I grab it out of her hands and put it back in its place.

"Sheesh. Sorry."

Bosca walks up. *Please don't say anything. I don't want her to know.* "Eve's paintings were burned in Friday's fire."

Great.

"Oh my God," she says, her hand to her mouth. "How awful."

I stop and look at her. Is she being sincere?

"It's like you can't catch a break. One bad thing after another."

Nope. Still snarky Vivian.

"Come." Antonio guides her away from the table. "Let her do her work. You do yours."

16

Danny

The light-rail powers down twice on the way home. Just stops dead on the tracks. It makes me think again about the grocery store.

"I met this girl." The train stutters forward, shifting everyone on board.

Germ grins. "Of course you did."

"At Abbot's. She acted like she knew me."

"Did she?"

I shrug.

"Well, did you get her name?"

"The power went out."

He laughs. "You can't talk to a girl in the dark?"

"Shut up. I'm serious. The lights went out, and she was gone."

"Maybe she was a ghost."

"In a grocery store?"

"You never know," he says. "But I wouldn't sweat it. I'm sure there'll be another girl along any minute."

I shove his head. He pulls his arm back to swing at me, but I point at my bruise. "Don't, man. You'll give me brain damage." He swings anyway. And misses.

The train powers down a third time. Germ groans. "This sucks."

"Better than what they're going through over at the blast site."

"No kidding," he says, his voice low. "They're saying everything's fried. Electricity. Traffic lights. Even cars blitzed out."

I want to ask him more about Friday, but don't dare. Not only could it tip him off that I'm not who he thinks I am, but in this Phoenix you never knows who's listening.

When the doors open, we ditch the train, walking along the tracks until we reach a shopping area closer to the harbor. Trees line the street, and a winding sidewalk runs along the front of stores and restaurants. The sun is trying hard to make an appearance, but clouds keep getting in the way. Germ stops outside West Coast Espresso and leans back against a tree, one foot on the trunk. Roots push through cracks in the concrete, making the slabs uneven, like they're moving on slow-motion waves. Cars stop and go at the traffic light. A couple of workers, one high up in a cherry picker, tinker with the power lines. People sit at tables outside the coffee shop. "We got time," he says. "Wanna do some digging?"

"Uh . . . sure." Whatever that means.

"Think we can do it without getting caught?" He looks at the tables. One woman is reading a book. Another sits with her back to us.

"Probably."

"You want the nab?"

"No, you go ahead." I have no idea what he's talking about.

Germ looks down the street. When there's a break in traffic, he walks over to a garbage can at the edge of the coffee shop patio and reaches under its lip while pretending to throw something away. He walks back, flashing something in his hand before shoving it into his pocket. He leans against the tree again. "You know, after this Skylar thing goes live, there'll be no more hiding. Like, at all."

My eyes move to the camera mounted on the roof of the coffee shop, pointed toward the intersection. "We've already got cameras everywhere, watching us."

"Yeah, but they're saying Skylar will be like Spectrum on steroids."

Another puzzle piece falls into place. The cameras are Spectrum.

"You know what we should do?" He glances over his shoulder. "Before Skylar goes live, we should totally bomb the city."

"What?" A chill runs up my neck.

"You know." He makes a *Duh* face and holds his hand out like he's using a spray can.

"Oh. I thought you meant . . ." With my own hands I make an explosion.

"RD's got that covered." He looks past me toward the coffee shop. "We'd have to do something everyone would see."

"Commandeer a billboard?"

"That'd definitely get noticed."

I scan the fronts of the buildings, seeing them like blank slates instead of walls. "Eye level would be better."

Germ follows to where I'm looking. "We'd totally get caught."

"What if we were invisible?"

He laughs.

"No, I'm serious." I nod at the workers up on the power lines. "What if we blended in?"

Germ grins. "That would be awesome. But"—he shakes his head—"risky, man."

Dad's words come back to me *No more taking risks. Keep your head down.*

Germ looks over at the patio again. One of the women is gone. The other still has her back to us. After another quick glance over his shoulder, he reaches into his pocket and pulls out a rectangular box smaller than his palm. It has a strip of magnet across the back. He slides open the hatch with his thumb. Inside is a flash drive. He tips it out and holds his hand open for us both to see. "Is that a seven or a nine?"

A piece of paper with letters and numbers scribbled on it is taped to the back of the drive. "Looks like a nine," I say. "See the loop?"

He tucks it into his other front pocket. "So, that means what? Thunderbird and . . . Fifty-First?"

"Sounds right." I have no clue.

"That'd be the Parkside drop, over by the Canal Bridge. Too bad we don't have any paint." He hands me the box. "Your turn."

"I don't have anything to throw away."

He makes a face. "Pretend."

Right. Because I'm great at that.

I take a step toward the garbage can and he pulls me back, his eyes wide. A patrol car rolls by. "What are you doing? You're gonna get us caught."

The woman stands up from the table and goes inside the shop. I check to make sure the coast is clear, then stride over to the can and slip the box under the lip. My method isn't as smooth as Germ's, but it gets the job done.

"Come on," he says. "Let's unload this thing." We walk to the next intersection and take a right into a neighborhood. It looks older, with smaller houses and huge trees. This Phoenix is so green it almost hurts my eyes. And not a single cactus in sight.

"You know who could totally make us invisible?" Germ says. "M."

I catch myself from asking, *Who?*

We walk another twenty minutes or so down the road before hanging a left. At the third house on the right, Germ stops. I keep an eye out while he reaches into the bushes at the base of the mailbox. He pulls out a second box. Inside is a piece of paper. He swaps it with the drive from the coffee shop, then puts the box back into the bushes. It takes seconds.

"You know what else Skylar's gonna do?" Germ asks when we're farther down the street. "It's gonna ruin digging. We won't be able to do this anymore. No more passing along unfiltered information. No more sharing ideas or messages. First it was computers and phones. Then the cameras and street mics. They won't stop until they know everything we say and do."

I kick a rock down the sidewalk. "You sound like my dad."

"I know," he says, kicking the same rock again. "I sound like mine, too."

At the intersection we make a right. There's the park-and-ride and Germ's waiting car. "Speaking of M . . ." He pulls the paper out of his pocket and hands it to me. It's random letters and numbers. I don't have a clue what it means.

But I fake it. "Cool."

17

EEVEE

My phone rings as I'm walking to meet Warren at the Archives. It's Dad. I consider not answering, but the last time I tried to ignore him, security tracked me down in the middle of civics class. So embarrassing. And that was *before* we were under a terrorism watch.

"Hi, Dad."

"How's my girl? Did the shipment of remains—"

"'Remains'? Geez, Dad."

"Sorry." He clears his throat. "What I meant was, how are you doing?"

"As good as can be expected, I guess." I dodge students on the sidewalk. "Considering I've been sorting through the burned and shredded *remains* of my soul."

He sighs. "Anything salvageable?"

"Of my soul?"

"Of your paintings." He's losing patience with me.

I scale back the melodrama and tell him the truth. "I found

most of the pieces of one and still have a heap of scraps to sift through." Saying it out loud makes the truth of it sink in even more.

"Can you put the one back together?"

"Sure. If I want my entry to look like something out of *Frankenstein*." My feet stop in their tracks. An idea takes shape in my mind.

He's quiet a moment, then says, "This must be very difficult. Your mother and I, we just want you to know we're here and supporting you."

"Thanks." I start walking again. I'm going to be so late for our study session.

"See you on Friday?".

"What's Friday?"

"The Stand Up to Terror event."

"Where is—"

"Richard will send you the details. Listen, I have to take another call. Good luck with the paintings, honey."

Even after he's hung up, I keep walking with the phone to my ear. Guess I'll see him on Friday.

The Archives are in an old brick building at the heart of campus. Doric columns rise on either side of the double oak doors. Walking in, I'm greeted with the smells of musty paper and dust. My flip-flops make slapping noises in the entryway, so I tiptoe past a wall of student artwork, toward our meeting place. Warren is already sitting at the table reading, his glasses up on his forehead.

"You look different without your lab coat."

"I'm in disguise."

"What are you, a spy?"

He holds a finger to his lips. "Shhh. I'm casing out the guy behind you."

I look. There is no guy behind me.

He smirks.

"I'll go find someone else to study with if you're not careful."

"You'll fail science."

I cross my arms. "And you'll fail art history."

"Touché." He moves his notebooks so I can set my stuff down.

We've been meeting for a couple of months now, and I still don't know what to make of him. He's goofy, arrogant and slightly antisocial. And he wears ankle pants. He's also super smart and makes me laugh. We're an oddball pairing. The genius and the artist. Like Einstein and Picasso. We're also a strangely successful pairing, given that we met through the student message board. Being the governor's daughter complicates everything—friendships, relationships. I find it best to keep people at arm's length. But when I saw the ad about swapping science help for art history, it just kind of made sense.

I take the chair across from him and pull my science notes out of my bag. "You didn't tell me you were part of the Skylar team."

"There are lots of things I don't tell you." He leans forward. "So, did you figure it out?"

"We should get to work."

He rolls his eyes. "But the code was so easy."

It takes me a while to find the note he passed to me at the press conference. I finally find it in my bag, smashed between a binder and a biography of Rembrandt. "I thought it was going to be something important." I toss it on the table.

He looks left and right, then whispers, "It is important."

"It's just letters and numbers."

"Those letters and numbers could change your life." He raises an eyebrow and nods slowly.

"Yeah, well, you could have changed my life by getting me in trouble. If my dad had seen you passing me a note—"

He waves away my complaint. "You're just stalling now."

"Fine." I unfold the note and read it again. And again. Then shake my head. "Still don't get it."

He falls back in his chair. "You're hopeless as a spy."

"News flash: I'm not trying to be a *spy*." I flop my science binder open and pull out my study guide. "I'm trying to be an *artist* who can pass her science class."

"Not nearly as fun."

Last month I helped him prepare for his test on art during the Cold War, when the movement toward protecting Americans from countercultural ideas began. He aced it, of course, because he had me in his corner. Now I'm the one who needs help. This unit on atoms is just not meshing. It's not that I'm bad at science. It's just that my brain works better with images than words, and Warren is really good at translating scientific jargon into pictures. "We really should get started." I slide my study guide across the table.

"First promise you'll try to figure out the code."

"Fine." I raise my right hand. "I promise. Now, can we . . . ?"

He moves his glasses down onto his face and looks over the study guide, muttering words as he reads. "Matter . . . atoms . . . polarity . . ." He sets it down. "Electromagnetic repulsion. Fascinating stuff."

"Enlighten me, Einstein."

"Atoms are ninety-nine percent empty space. They get their shape from the negatively charged electrons spinning around the nucleus. Now, the human body is made up of approximately seven octillion atoms—"

"That's not a word."

"Yes it is. Seven octillion atoms, which means you are mostly empty space."

"*You're* mostly empty space."

He scowls. "Pay attention. Everything is made of atoms, so everything is mostly nothing. Empty space. And that means you're not actually sitting on that chair."

"Is this that thing where you're just showing off how much you know? Or does this actually have to do with my test?"

"Listen." He sticks out his hands like he's holding an invisible ball. "The closer atoms are together, the more they repulse each other. Like when you try to force magnets to touch pole to pole. You feel that resisting force between them, right? So, the same thing is happening right now between your butt and that chair. It feels like you're sitting, but you're actually floating above it."

"Suspended by the repulsion of my seven—what was it?"

"Octillion."

"Seven *octillion* atoms."

"Exactly. Which means there isn't really such a thing as

touching." He puts his hand flat on the table. "I'm not actually touching this. There is an infinitesimal amount of space between the atoms of the desk and the atoms of my hand."

"But you feel it."

"And yet, I'm still not *actually* touching it."

He continues working his way through the concepts, and forty minutes later, I feel like I have enough of a grasp to take the test.

"Coulomb's law is the foundation of electromagnetism. And electromagnetism is the foundation of the new Skylar system." He hands me the study guide. "Coincidence?"

I think back to the explanation they gave during the DART demo, before Nina passed that wand over my head. "You mean, you think we're studying this stuff now because of that?"

He gives a small shrug. "I wouldn't be surprised if you start to see it cropping up more and more. Introduce an idea, then disseminate it through the populace until it becomes a new norm." He looks at his watch and begins packing up his things. "That's how I'd do it, at least."

I gather up my stuff, too. "If you're such a skeptic, why do you work for them?"

"I don't work for them." He zips up his backpack. "I'm an intern."

"You know what I mean."

He thinks a moment, then says, "Let's just say I'm doing my part to ensure the promise of our future." He grins, knowing I'd recognize the line from Dad's speech. "Seriously, though, it's the ultimate gig for a science student. Huge opportunity.

Security systems are just one aspect of DART. There are lots of programs people don't know about. Stealth technologies. Microbiological weaponry. You name it."

"Do you work on those, too?"

"If I told you that, I'd have to kill you." He slings his backpack over his shoulder and we walk together toward the exit.

He stops at the art wall, in front of a small painting of a rose. "Is this one of yours?"

"Yes." I'm still not happy with the way I painted the shadows beneath the petals.

"You know what you should do? Paint mash-ups of art and science." He crashes his hands together like an implosion. "That would be cool."

"Probably wouldn't get approved."

"Approved shmooved." He holds open the door and we walk out into warm midday air.

"Until next time, Eevee Solomon." He makes an exaggerated bow and saunters down the sidewalk. When he's almost out of earshot, he turns and yells, "Don't forget the note!"

18

Danny

The school welding shop roars with dozens of motors and machines running at once. Germ guides a length of metal tubing through the roller. It winds around in a wide arc. When it's done, he passes it to me and starts on the next one. I measure and mark two and a half feet, then make the cut using the band saw. My brain tells me over and over to pay attention, but the rattle of the machine puts me in a kind of trance. My thoughts spin like the blade, on an endless loop.

This morning, three more girls stopped to talk to me when I got to school. That's five so far. Definitely a new record. That never happens to me back home, unless you count them calling me a burnout or a loser. Still, I would trade all the girls I've ever talked to in either world for the chance to see the grocery store girl again.

"Hey!" Germ's voice snaps me out of my daze. He slides the last piece on the table and measures the tile we've chosen for the top. "Earth to Ogden."

I switch the machine off and carry the cut pieces over to the worktable.

"You looked like you were trying to lose a finger," he says. "You okay?"

"Zoned out for a sec."

The teacher, a wiry guy with a Fu Manchu mustache, gave us an hour to create a stable structure. Other teams are building toolboxes, racks. Looks like one team is making a bench. We chose a table. And so far, so good. I've never done this kind of stuff before, and I'm watching Germ for cues, but it seems like I've got the hang of it. Like it comes naturally. I pull off my work gloves to wipe the sweat from under my safety goggles. My hands are grimy, but it's a satisfying grunge. It feels right.

If Palo Brea were more like this, I probably wouldn't ditch so much. Less lecturing, more doing. And doing real stuff, especially.

"We still on for tonight?" Germ grabs his welding helmet. I grab mine, too, and slip the band onto my head, wincing when it rubs the bruise.

"Yep." I line up a length of the metal tubing with the upside-down table frame and flip my visor down. Germ leans in and takes the first weld. My visor window reacts to the bright glow, then clears so I can see. The metal sizzles and pops as he weaves the wire through the seam. I watch him closely, studying how he moves. When the leg is secured all around, he flips his helmet up and blows on the welder tip like it's the barrel of a gun. Then it's my turn.

We trade places and I take a deep breath while he lines up

the next leg. When he gives me the nod, I set the welder tip in place and flip my helmet down. I press the trigger, but the wire misses the metal and spools out. A total dud. I groan and press the tip closer into the corner where the leg meets the frame. Hold my breath and press the trigger again. This time it catches, sticking to the metal and melting the two pieces into one. I watch the orange glow through my visor and stitch the wand like Germ did, guiding it around the table leg. When I reach the end, I pull the welder away, flip up my visor and watch the weld cool from orange to black. It isn't as pretty as Germ's work, but hopefully it's as good as Danny's.

19

EEVEE

Wednesday before civics class, I take a break and sit outside under a eucalyptus tree on the lawn next to my dorm, Mc-Connell Hall. The day looks colder than it actually is. From my bag I pull an apple and Warren's super secret spy note. It's become a welcome distraction from everything going on.

The last one he gave me was way easier: a backward number 1, a square, and a backward 2. *Back to square one.* This puzzle, though, has me stumped.

I take a bite of apple and read through it again.

my573ry c45713 w3d 2130

I look out across the lawn, watch a grackle hop by and read it again. Maybe if I let my eyes go unfocused, it'll pop out at me? No. I take another bite of apple and think about *Confidante* instead.

Ever since Dad mentioned putting it back together, my

brain's been noodling around with an idea. Even if I could glue it back together with resin or PVA, the pieces are damaged beyond restoration. But what if I do something different? Stitch them together, maybe, or wire them into place. It wouldn't be anything I could submit to the jury, but it might be cool to have for my own collection.

The bell rings and students stream out onto the sidewalks. Time to get to class. I take a last bite and look down at the note.

Something clicks.

The second letter-number combination is a word.

Castle.

The numbers are letters.

Mystery. Castle.

What's a mystery castle? And why is Warren telling me about it in code?

●

The silence of the library feels louder than the racket of the school hallways. Civics is happening in a lecture hall on the other side of the building, but I decided to come here instead. The note is now burning a hole in my pocket. I'll worry about what I missed in class later. I walk down the carpeted steps into the cocoon of velvet and mahogany and move through the towering shelves of books toward the information desk. The librarian looks at me over her readers. "May I help you?"

I keep my voice low. "This is a strange question, but have you ever heard of something called a mystery castle?"

"Is it in Phoenix?"

"I don't know."

"Have you searched online?"

"No." Too risky. But not if she does the searching for me.

"Let me run a keyword search through our collections first."

"Thanks."

She types on her keyboard, hits ENTER and scans the screen. "Here we are." In perfect script, she writes the location of the book on a slip of paper. "If this doesn't turn out to be what you're looking for, let me know." She slides the paper across the desk.

"Thank you." I read the notation. Another code to decipher: *979.1 TIMESPA—Adult—Book.*

"The history section begins four stacks to your right. Toward the end."

I thank her again and walk through the shelves, reading titles and reference numbers as I go. Now and then I step over a student sitting on the floor, engrossed in reading. Finally, I see the 900 section. I trace the reference numbers on the spines, then crouch to the lowest shelf and find it. *A History of Architecture in Arizona.* I set my bag on the floor and sit down.

The book is old. The pages are yellowed and have that stale smell of time and too many fingers turning them. The table of contents reveals nothing, so I go to the index and search through the Cs. *Carnival. Cars. Castle.*

Castle, Mystery, 81.

I flip to the page and read.

> *In the '40s, a man moved to Phoenix because of health problems. He had a lung disease that would be helped by the salt air. He*

didn't have enough money to move his family, so he came here alone. Every day he missed them, especially his daughter. With what money he had, he bought some land at the foot of South Mountain and built his daughter a castle out of rocks, bottles, scraps of anything he could find. One day she'd come to live with him, and when she did, she would live in a castle. He died, though, before he ever saw that day come.

Sepia-toned photos show the odd formations of the building. Pillars of rock, windows of multicolored bits of glass. What a strange place.

I pull the note out and read it again. *Mystery castle.* If the *3s* are *Es,* then *w3d* means *wed. Wednesday.*

That's today.

If *5s* are *Ss,* then maybe *2s* are *Zs.* So 2130 means . . . *zieo?* That can't be right. Maybe they're just numbers. An address? No. A time. Military time: 2130 is 9:30 p.m.

Mystery Castle Wed 9:30 p.m.

This isn't a puzzle. It's a coded invitation. But why?

Because it's a secret.

I quickly fold the note and look over my shoulder, but there are only books staring back. I bury the paper deep inside my bag and return the book to its place on the shelf. If I check it out, my name will be associated with it. It's a long shot that anyone would make the connection, but why take the risk?

"Was the book helpful?" The librarian's question startles me when I pass her desk.

"Um"—I make a sad face—"no, it wasn't quite what I was looking for."

"Do you want to try online?" She points at her computer.

"No." I back away. "That's okay. It doesn't really matter."

"Watch out for the—"

I bump into a cart and yelp so loud everyone stares at me. I straighten the toppled books and whisper, "Sorry," before rushing for the doors. So much for not drawing attention to myself.

20

Danny

After school, Germ comes over to work on the secret plan to make our mark on the city before Skylar goes live. Too stuffed from dinner to move, I lie on the bed and flip through the drawings in Danny's sketchbook. Germ sprawls out on the floor, pencil in his teeth, staring at the ceiling. His eyes move when he thinks. "The thing is, we have to make sure no one recognizes our work. I mean, you're known for your faces. I'm known for my letters."

"You are?"

He lifts his head off the floor and snaps, "Yes."

Oops. "Just messing with you, man."

The sketchbook is full of people, animals, monsters. I turn a page and suck in my breath. It's *her*. Dark hair, bright eyes. My throat goes tight. Should I ask Germ who she is?

He mutters something I can't understand.

"What?"

He takes the pencil out of his teeth. "Stencils." He sits

up on his elbows. "What if we do stencils? Not as fun as free-form, but we can paint it quickly and no one will know it's us."

"I don't remember the last time I used a stencil," I say, still staring at her.

"Dude, we used them last week at the mall." He raises his eyebrow. "Still can't remember?"

I shake my head.

He taps a rhythm on the floor and stares at me. Then he looks back at the ceiling. "The hard part is deciding what to make."

"Well . . ." I set the sketchbook aside and stretch my legs up the wall so my head falls back over the edge of the bed. "What do we want to say?"

He drums the pencil. "That Skylar is bad."

"'Skylar is the devil'?"

"A devil face with *Skylar* over the eyes?"

"A red circle with *Skylar* crossed out?"

We both go quiet. What *are* we trying to say? I try to think up the right image. My mind flashes to the time Brent caught me sneaking into the foster home after being out all night. He was waiting for me in my room. Leapt out of the dark and pounded the crap out of me. "This is about control," I say, still seeing his fists flying. "When you're afraid, you're easily controlled."

"Maybe something like 'Don't be afraid'?"

"'Don't let them control you'?"

"'Stop giving them control'?"

"How about 'Fear equals control'?"

"That's good." He turns to a blank page in his notebook and starts sketching. "*Equals* like an equal sign?"

"Yeah. Don't you think?"

He nods. I watch his pencil pull lines across the paper. Each one is exact, fitting with the next. He really is good.

In no time flat, he's done. "Something like this?"

The word *fear* is shaky, like the letters are scared. Two thick parallel lines make the equal sign. And the word *control* is heavy and solid, with cracks breaking the invisible ground beneath it.

"Dude." I sit up and my head spins. "That is awesome."

He sets the paper down. "What if we get caught?"

"But we've done this with RD." I tread carefully. "Right?"

"This feels different." He grasps his elbows around his knees. "They always had our back, you know? With this, we'll be on our own."

"They didn't on Friday when we almost got blown up."

"Good point." He shakes his head. "Listen, we can't do this anywhere near my dad's beat, deal?"

"Your dad is a cop?!" It's out of my mouth before I realize what I've done.

Germ's face changes from confusion to anger. He stands up and throws the pencil to the floor. "That's it. What the hell is wrong with you?"

"Nothing." I try to shrug it off.

"Huh-uh. Something's not right. Start talking."

My mind scrambles to come up with an excuse, but when you're best friends with someone the way Danny is best friends with Germ, you know things like the fact that his dad is a cop.

I run my hand over my too-short hair and stare at the FEAR = CONTROL sign.

I have to tell him.

"I'm not Danny," I say, avoiding his eyes. "I look like him, but I'm not. I mean, I am, but not the Danny you know. Something happened and I jumped here from another world. Like this one, only not."

I sound like a crazy person.

He stares at me for a long time, then smirks. "This is a joke, right?"

I shake my head.

"Come on, man," he says. "It isn't even a good one. At least say you're an alien body snatcher or something."

I just look at him until he scoffs again. "So next you're gonna tell me the Danny I know is . . . where? Sucked into a black hole?"

"Maybe?"

He holds up his hands. "Okay, enough. I get it. Ha ha."

"I'm not joking." Even though Germ is freaking out, it actually feels good telling someone.

"Prove it."

"How?"

"I don't know." He crosses his arms. "Tell me about where you're from. Tell me who I am there."

I swallow. "We aren't friends . . . where I'm from."

"What?!" His mouth hangs open.

"It's totally different there. My, um . . ." I stare at the floor. The good feeling I had is gone, replaced by a mix of panic and grief. "My parents died when I was eleven. I live in a foster home with four other kids. The youngest is Benny. He's five. The place is a shithole. Brent's always drunk. Suzy does what she can to keep him off us, but he's mean. The truth is, I don't really have any friends there. Not like . . . this."

When I look at Germ again, he's backed up almost to the door. "And this is why you don't remember stuff?"

"Yeah, I'm pretty lost. I don't get half the things you talk about." I shrug. "It wasn't me who experienced them. Listen, I'll totally understand if you leave," I lie.

Neither of us moves. Silence swallows the room.

After what feels like forever, he says, "Well, you're doing a good job impersonating him. Almost." He takes a step forward. "I can catch you up on what you should know." He picks up the notebook. "But one thing you gotta work on is your confidence. Nothing rattles Danny." He sits again in the same spot on the floor. "And don't even ask me to help with that, because I sure as hell don't know how."

I sit on the edge of the bed. "Confidence. Okay. Anything else?"

"Yeah," Germ says, picking up the pencil. "Lighten up. I know the world's gone to crap, but we still gotta have a good time."

We work into the night coming up with ideas and turning them into stencils. Empty chip bags and soda cans litter the floor. Germ sits surrounded by scraps cut from the poster board we found in Mom's craft supplies. I practice drawing letters in a notebook. Now that he knows my secret, there's no pressure to pretend I'm good at this. But I'm surprised—we both are, really—that I'm actually not bad. Kind of like the welding. Germ thinks it's muscle memory.

"No *ocean*?" He uses the X-acto to slice along the lines of an eye. "I can't even wrap my brain around that. So you can drive straight to California?"

"I haven't, but yeah. Arizona ends and California begins."

"Is California the same? I mean, the cities and stuff?"

I shrug. "No idea. Never been there. Mine or yours."

"You should go sometime. It's cool. Danny's been there a bunch of times with his dad." He looks up at me. "I mean your dad." He shakes his head again and looks down at his work. "Are you going to tell them?"

"My parents? I don't know what to say."

"How about what you said to me?" He pops a letter out of the poster board.

"Yeah, and you just about walked out."

"But I didn't. And they're your parents. They can handle it."

"I'll think about it." I set down my pencil and shake out my hand. "What changed your mind about leaving?"

He doesn't answer right away. Finally, he says, "All that stuff you said about your life there? If he's living in that—the Danny I know—what kind of asshole would I be to give up on him here?" He looks up. "And if he comes back, I don't want him to think I abandoned him, you know?"

I nod. There's nothing more to say.

Germ changes the subject. "So how do you think it happened? The jumping."

"No idea." I pick up the pencil again and sketch a face, the mouth open and screaming.

"Maybe it was a time tunnel." Germ shifts the angle of his poster and leans over it.

"What's a time tunnel?"

"I don't know, but it sounds cool. You said it was like a tunnel, right?"

"Yeah." I open my mouth like I'm screaming and realize the eyes in my sketch should be closed. "But it wasn't really solid. More like just swirling."

"Like clouds?"

"Kinda. It was dark, with different shades of black."

Germ looks at me through a hole he cut. "It's like something from a science fiction movie. *Danny and the Time Tunnel of Zangarthum.*"

I laugh, brushing eraser crumbs away. "Zangar—what?"

"I don't know. It sounded better than Phoenix." He goes back to cutting. *"Danny and the Time Vortex of Doom."*

"Doom?"

"Always sounds better if there's doom."

I hold up the notebook for him to see.

"Looks good." Germ pops another hole out of the stencil.

I set the notebook down. "Thing is, it's not really like time travel, is it? The dates are the same. Left there on Friday, got here on Friday. It's like I just . . . switched Phoenixes."

"Well, that's gonna sound really lame as a movie title. *Danny: The Guy Who Switched Phoenixes. Danny and the Phoenix Switch of Doom.*"

"Sure is a lot of doom."

"Doom sells, man. You want people to see your movie? You gotta use the word *doom*." He holds up the finished stencil. "Speaking of, we should probably get going."

"What?" I look at the clock on the desk. It's 9:30. "Where?"

"Didn't you read the note?" He stands up and pulls on his skullcap.

"You mean that paper you showed me when we were out digging? I have no idea what that said."

He laughs. "Well, this should be fun."

"You're not going to tell me?"

"Nope." He grins. "Put on a hat."

I scowl at him and pull a baseball cap out of the closet. "Come on."

If there's one thing I know how to do, it's climb out of windows. At the foster home, I used them more than I used the front door.

"Where are we going?" I whisper once we're outside. I start to walk across the yard toward the road, but Germ grabs my sleeve. He points at the streetlights and shakes his head. "This is going to be so much easier when you get a clue."

We creep along the front of my house, through the side gate and across the backyard to the alley. Keeping to the shadows, we slink from garbage can to garbage can. The air feels damp, heavy. At the end of the alley, Germ stops me with his hand. He pulls his keys out of his pocket and flashes a small light on the key chain once. Down the street, headlights flash twice and go dark. Germ looks both ways and we leave the shadows for the road.

Parked in the darkness is the strangest vehicle I've ever

seen. Tiny cab and a bed lined with slats, like a vegetable truck or something, painted black and rigged with oversize tires. Germ jumps into the back, and I follow. There are eight or so people sitting there. They say *hi* like they know me, shake my hand, bump my fist.

Without a sound, the truck starts moving. No engine noise. Is it electric? Like a silent black ship, we sail through the streets, stopping now and again for others to join or to wait for a patrol car to pass. It's after curfew and the streets are empty. No one in the back says a word.

As the truck continues southeast, the city changes from cookie-cutter houses to double-wides. Streetlights move farther apart. We pass a lonely and run-down taco stand: TWO FISH TACOS FOR $3.50. And then we leave the streets behind. Trade paved roads for dirt. Whispers kick up in the dark. Germ leans toward me and says in a low voice, "Wonder if anyone from RD will show."

"*Where* are you taking us?" I hiss.

"Castle. You'll see." He rests his head back on a wooden slat. "If Neil's there, I'm gonna . . ." He pounds his fist into his hand.

The farther we drive, the bumpier the road gets. At one point we hit something big, a boulder or a downed tree maybe, and everyone in the back jostles. Laughter rises from the darkness.

"That's gonna hurt."

"Better not get stranded out here."

"We'll make you push."

"Almost there now."

"Look."

The truck's lights flash on for a second. A huge mountain stands before us, surrounded by a sea of cars. The truck comes to a stop.

I turn to ask Germ where we are, but he's already climbing out.

Thumping bass drones through the night air. We walk with the others toward a strange building at the base of the mountain. Our feet raise dust that the breeze quickly carries away. Germ claps me on the back. "Tonight is going to be out of this world."

21

EEVEE

Jonas slows as he approaches the checkpoint, and reaches one hand back toward me. I give him my ID and credentials, just in case. We shouldn't need them since the car has political plates, but you never know.

He'd had no reaction when I told him where to take me. And I acted like it was no big deal. Now that we're on our way, though, my heart feels like it's going to pound right out of my chest. There's a chance he'll tell Dad, but maybe he won't, too. It's not the first time he's driven me to an event on my own. A date once, even. And if things go really badly, I can always rat out Warren.

Jonas rolls down the window, but the military guys wave him on. Behold, the power of political status. The car accelerates and we're on our way again, driving away from the city. I lean my head against the window to look at the sky. Too many clouds to see the stars tonight. Even if it were clear, Phoenix has so much light pollution, you can only see a couple of the brightest ones anyway. I roll down the window for a better look, but the wind does a number on my hair, so I roll it back up.

Jonas looks at me in the rearview. "We aren't going Outbound, are we?"

I overlaugh at the question. "Don't be silly. Outbound is on the *other* side of South Mountain." I chew on my lip. He's definitely going to tell Dad.

The last business—a fish taco stand—gives way to ramshackle houses and trailers, then nothing. I've never been this far before. Never had reason to.

The car bumps over the end of the road and the headlights fill with dust. Jonas slows to avoid boulders and dips. This is crazy. We're going to blow a tire and get mugged out here. I shouldn't have worn heels. Or maybe I can use one to stab out someone's eye if I need to.

Please don't let me need to.

He slows to a stop. The engine idles and dust swirls in the headlights. "Is that it?"

I lean forward to look through the windshield. At the base of the mountain stands the same strange rock structure I saw in the book at the library.

The Mystery Castle.

"Yes."

Jonas's face in the rearview is unimpressed. "I can't get any closer than this."

"It's okay. I'll walk."

He turns off the engine and goes around to open my door. "I'll see you to the entrance."

"You don't have to."

He holds out his hand and I take it. Thumping bass mingles with the dust. A rave? Disappointment washes over me.

As we near the entrance, the music grows louder. Now and then a voice rises above the noise. Jonas clears his throat. Is it in judgment or because he's choking on dust? I stumble over a rock and he grabs my hand to keep me from falling down.

"Thanks."

He stops at the chain-link fence encircling the castle and waits for me to enter first.

"I can manage from here."

He looks up at the castle, the rising rock pillars and mountain beyond. "Text me a half hour before you want to leave. I'll meet you back here."

I check my pocket to make sure my phone is there. "Thank you."

He disappears into the dust and darkness. I turn to face the noise and unknown.

The Mystery Castle grows out of the ground, walls and arches made of stone from the surrounding foothills. Movements from the shadows catch my eye. I'm not alone in the courtyard between the fence and the castle. I walk toward the lights, and the music grows louder. Shallow steps lead past a high wall of stacked and mortared stones. I slide my hand along the smooth and jagged surfaces. This place is like something from my dreams. If only I had my drawing pad and charcoals. The wall curves, wrapping around to the right. Music thumps through me, a constant percussion in my bones. I step through the gap where the wall ends, and stop. An inner courtyard opens before me, carved out of the mountain. Hundreds of bodies move with the beat, strobes and lasers skating across skin and stone. The hair on my arms stands on end. Who are they? Where did they all come from?

A woman slides through the gap behind me and melts into the movement. Through the laser lights and raised-up hands I see the source of the music: a makeshift DJ table loaded with equipment. Two guys, one with headphones draped around his neck, stand behind the table talking, their shadows cast against the walls.

I do a double take.

The one with the headphones is Warren.

I ease myself along, dodging dancers and trying not to step on toes. The place is huge. And old. I'm sure officials know it's here, but do they know it's being used for *this*? I look back toward the entrance, imagining military personnel charging through, and a shiver runs down my neck. I shake the thought away and focus on the ravers instead. The music shifts, transitions, and a new beat, faster, takes over. Everyone follows. The music presses into me. I can't keep my body from moving in time.

Finally, I make it to the DJ stand. Warren sways as his hands turn dials, push buttons. He holds one side of the headphones against his ear, then lets them fall to his neck again. Gone is my oddball study partner. This Warren's jeans are skinny, his shirt striped like a cat. Perched on his head is a pair of goggles. Now and again the lenses catch the lights. This Warren is . . . cool. The guy he's talking to is thin as a pole and decked out head to toe in black. Even his hair, which is long and slicked back. If it weren't for the lasers and strobes, he'd blend right into the night.

The thin guy nods toward me. Warren turns and smiles wide. He shouts, "You figured it out."

"Why am I here?" My own voice doesn't even dent the noise. I can tell he didn't hear me. He says something to the thin guy, who then glares at me. He gives Warren a nod and walks off the stage. I try again, shouting, "Why am I here?" but Warren holds up a finger, pulls the headphones onto his head and goes to work. He loses himself in the music, eyes closed, body jerking in a dance that is both erratic and infectious. Then he focuses again, pressing buttons and moving levers. The music morphs and a hundred arms go into the air. He's running the show, watching the crowd with a smile on his face. He presses a button and steps away from the table. At the front of the stage, a single column of laser light fans out into fifteen. Each one a different color, they shoot up into the sky.

He stands behind them, holding his hands out flat at his waist. His head bobs with the music as he slides his left hand into a beam of light, cutting it off midstream. His palm lights up yellow and an eerie undercurrent rises in the music. He pulls his left hand back and slides the right forward. His hand glows blue and the music shifts again. Ghostly voices emerge. He holds his right hand there, his body one with the beat, then slides it out and places the left one in. I watch him, mesmerized. He's creating music with light.

Without looking, he reaches out to me, takes my hand and stretches it into the light. My palm glows purple and the music shifts. He picks up my other hand, moves it forward into blue.

Then he holds out both of his own hands at me like, *Here you go,* and steps back with a bow. The show is mine. Panic flickers inside me, but I close my eyes and let the music overwhelm me until my whole body buzzes. I open my eyes again and look at the beams of light. Move my hand to the green before switching back to the purple. The lasers are programmed with chords, pedal tones. I know this stuff like, well, like the back of my hand. I move through a progression of chords, creating a new composition. Each time the music shifts, the crowd follows. It's like magic. My skin rises in gooseflesh as an old flame awakens in me. This is how music should feel. This music is alive.

I'm alive.

Warren taps me on the shoulder and rolls his hand like, *Keep going,* and walks back to the table. He transitions to a faster beat and I follow. Shouts go up from the crowd. Hundreds of bodies move in sync. I sway in time, creating a new chord progression, and look out over the faces appearing and disappearing in the crowd. I move my hand through the purple beam, and a single face catches my eye. My hands drop.

It's him.

The boy from the museum.

I watch the lights play across his face and remember the feeling of his lips on mine. Three times? Three random meetings? How is that possible?

Maybe they're not random.

I have to get over there. I have to see him. Between us churns a sea of people and no easy path. The way to reach him will have to be through.

22

Danny

Strobe lights flash across the castle walls. I've never seen anything like it. I've been to parties back home, but they were lame compared to this. Someone's parents go out of town and you hang out on their couch, listening to metal and getting high, wishing there were some girls around but too stoned to move. This place is alive. The music—stuff I'd never think of listening to—pulses through my body. It's like a whirlpool, pulling me in. I don't dance, but I can't keep still either.

Germ elbows me and points. He says something I can't hear and walks toward the far wall. As we move through the crowd, bodies slide up against me, slowing me down. If I lose Germ, I'll never find him again.

He approaches three guys. I've never seen them before, but when I finally catch up, they talk to me like we go way back.

"Mastermind is on fire tonight!" one shouts. He bounces his head with the beat and his stringy hair swishes over his eyes. Mastermind must be the DJ.

"So many people!" Germ shouts.

"Security was cake," a guy in a skull sweatshirt says. He must be dying. It's a gazillion degrees.

"Too easy," Stringy Hair Guy says.

Skull Guy bumps Germ with the back of his hand and points toward the corner by the DJ stage. A guy in a black coat leans against the wall.

Germ thumps me on the arm. "Okay?"

I missed whatever he said. "Yeah. Sure."

He walks through the crowd toward the guy. I try to follow, but he slips through an opening too quick and I lose him. I can't catch up. It's like walking in the ocean with waves crashing against me, pushing me back.

Just when I think I'm totally stuck, there's a break in the crowd. I step through and find myself face to face with her.

The girl from the grocery store.

How?

A smile spreads across her face, a dangerous look in her eye. She slides up to me, puts one hand around my neck and raises the other in the air. Her body is warm against mine. Everything falls away until it's just the two of us, swallowed up in the moment.

The music shifts and the droning bass buzzes through my chest like a swarm of bees. Pressure builds inside. This isn't the music anymore. It feels like there's a weight pressing down. Static takes over the beat. My eyes cloud and I blink against the darkness. Lungs burning, I open my mouth in an empty scream.

Then stars. I see stars. Cold air whispers against my skin.

Grass blades press into my hands. Everything is silent and I'm staring at the stars.

A face moves into view, hovering over me. Dark eyes peer into mine and long hair brushes against my arm. My name is on her lips but her voice is drowned out as the static swells and the darkness returns.

Falling fast, I land again—*wham!*—my feet hard on the castle floor, the strobes blinding my eyes. I cough and try to blink the crowd into focus.

She holds on to my arms. I watch her lips. *You okay?* They're the same lips I just saw—the same face but on another person in another world. I hang on to this beautiful girl like she's an anchor. Where was I? Why was she there with me?

Bodies press in, crash against us, break us apart. There's angry shouting, then fists flying. More fighting erupts as people get jostled and punches land. Holding her hand tight, I turn into the crowd, dodging fists and elbows, letting the force push us along toward the exit. Across the way, I see Germ deck a dark-haired guy in the face. The guy stumbles back before tackling Germ. Germ swings and hits a girl by accident. More people jump in to defend her. It's insane. The place is a shit show and I can't get close enough to help. The dark-haired guy staggers up the steps to the archway, Germ right on his tail. The crowd spills into the outer courtyard. I pull the girl close and we step into the stream of people surging toward the exit. In no time we're pushed out into the courtyard, too.

There's more room out here, not to mention air. People walk around dazed, blinking like they don't know how they got here. Some continue to fight; others fall down. Across the courtyard, Germ shoves the dark-haired guy to the ground. I run toward them, my hand still holding tight to hers.

"Admit it!" Germ yells. "You set us up!"

The guy rolls to dodge Germ's foot. "Wait!" Germ doesn't wait. He kicks him in the side and the guy curls into a ball. Whoever he is, he's got information, which means he won't be of any use if he's dead. I grab Germ's arms and hold him back.

"What are you doing? Let me go!" He tries to wrestle free but he's no match for me. "This asshole planned to have us killed!"

Surprised, I loosen my grip. The guy's almost to his feet when Germ knocks him down again. He shouts, "It wasn't us!" I catch a glimpse of his face before he holds up his hands to shield himself from another blow.

I *know* him.

Germ stops short. "Who was it, then?" His shoulders heave.

When he's sure Germ isn't going to hit him again, he pushes himself up and holds his side.

"Neil?" I step forward to get a clearer view.

"What?" He glares at me and touches his tongue to where his lip bleeds.

Neil Pratt. Palo Brea dropout. Sells drugs to people like me. In my old life.

He turns back to Germ. "I don't know. But it wasn't us."

"The directive sent us to the mall," Germ says.

"I know." Neil wipes the blood away. "I wrote it."

Germ clenches his fists. "But you didn't try to blow us up."

"You know how it works. Orders come from higher up. Friday was just supposed to be a message. Paint. That's all."

"Then who set off the bombs?"

Neil gives a weak smile and more blood oozes from his lip. "I was hoping you could tell me."

Germ scoffs. "It wasn't us."

"Yeah, well"—he touches his lip again—"it wasn't Red December either." He moves his tongue around in his mouth. "I think you broke my tooth."

"You're lucky I didn't break your face."

Neil sneers. "Oooh."

The roar of engines echoes across the courtyard and someone shouts, "Raid!" Light breaks over the wall. Armed guards in riot gear storm into the courtyard.

The girl grabs my arm and pulls me away. I look back to see Germ following us toward the dark of the mountain. When we reach the wall, she climbs up and over. The stones make for easy footholds. Before I know it, I'm over, too, running after her, with Germ behind. The ground rises as we approach the foothills. She stumbles, her shoes catching on the uneven gravel, and I grab her elbow to keep her from falling. The three of us slip into an alcove in the rock. Shouts carry up the slope from the castle below. Other ravers creep up the mountain and keep going. We watch them until they're swallowed by the night.

"Let's follow the Bounders," Germ whispers. "They'll know how to get out."

The girl pulls a phone from her pocket and dials, shielding the light of the screen. Footsteps approach. I take her hand, ready to bolt, but it isn't a guard who finds us. It's a skinny guy in a striped shirt and goggles.

"M," Germ whispers, waving him over.

This is M? He ducks down and crouches beside us. When he sees the girl, he smiles.

"Jonas?" Her voice is shaky. She covers her free ear and listens, then creeps forward to peek out of the alcove. "Yeah, I see you." She looks down the mountain. "I think so. Okay." She hangs up and continues to watch what the rest of us can't see. No one says anything. Finally, she motions us forward, whispering, "Come on."

We slink across the mountain. Below, the guards load the unluckies into vans and trucks. Looks like most of the revelers escaped. Our path takes us around the side, where the brush grows thicker. The girl leads the way, looking back now and then with wide eyes to make sure we're still with her. Soon the action is behind us.

When we get close to the flat of the foothills again, headlights blink. We break into an all-out run for the car, not stopping until we're inside with the doors closed. The car eases forward, lights off, turning away from the castle. The locks clamp down with a heavy *click*. No one says a word.

The driver is an older guy, balding. Wears a button-down shirt with a tie. He looks at the three of us—me, Germ and M—in the rearview. The girl sits in the passenger seat, rubbing her hands again and again on her jeans. Who is she? What kind of girl has her own driver?

"I'm assuming we're not heading to the Executive Tower?" the driver asks.

"No," she says. "School, please."

When the bumpy off-road becomes pavement, the driver

turns the headlights on and drives on nonchalantly, as if he hasn't just picked up four outlaw kids. Everyone relaxes a little.

Until we reach the roadblock.

As the car slows, I look out the windows, thinking up an escape plan. Our odds are better if we jump out the passenger side, but none of us can outrun the bullets. I realize I'm holding my breath.

For some reason, though, when the car is almost at a stop, the guard waves us on. The driver continues forward unfazed, accelerating at a normal rate even as my brain screams for him to gun it.

The girl glances back at me, then turns around again, not saying a word.

23

EEVEE

It isn't until we enter the school gates and we're past security that I feel myself breathe again. "Thanks," I whisper. Jonas doesn't answer. The guys in the backseat are so silent it's hard to believe they're there. How do they know each other? I puzzle over possible connections as I watch the trees lining the drive tick by.

Jonas pulls over in front of McConnell Hall and comes around to open my door. This isn't how I want the night to end, with so many unanswered questions. I turn in my seat to face Museum Boy.

"We keep meeting," he whispers. "Why?"

I shake my head. "I don't know."

The door opens and I start to get out. "Wait," he says. "What's your name?"

"Oh." I smile. "Eevee. What's yours?"

"Danny."

"Mine's Germ." His friend sticks his hand out between us. Danny pushes him back.

"That's an interesting name," I say, aware of Jonas waiting at my door. "Well, good night." I give a small wave to Warren, and a last look at Danny—hoping it really isn't the last—then exit the car.

I don't know what to say to Jonas except another "Thanks." He nods and walks back around to the driver's side. The car pulls from the curb and drives away.

When the taillights are out of view, I walk inside and take the stairs to the third floor. The hallway is so still. I try to move without making a sound as I pass my neighbors' doors. My key slips easily into the lock. Standing silent in the dark, I feel exhaustion begin to creep in. I flip on my desk light, half expecting my room to look different.

But it doesn't. All the safe paintings hang on the walls. My book bag and art smock lie where I left them. I exhale and sit on the edge of the bed.

Nothing has changed.

Everything has changed.

24

DANNY

Jonas drives to another building on campus, not far from where he dropped off Eevee, and stops at the curb. Germ and I get out, followed a moment later by M. "Thanks," he says, leaning in the passenger window. Jonas responds with a relaxed salute and drives away.

It's got to be at least 2 a.m. We walk in silence toward the building. M punches a code into a keypad and opens the door. Halfway down the hall, there's a staircase. We take it up three flights, our feet tapping on the concrete slabs, and make a left toward the far end of the building. His is the last room on the right.

He turns a key in the lock and holds up a hand for us to wait. The door opens a crack and there's a beeping sound. He slips his hand through the opening five times in a specific sequence—high, low, high, middle, high—and the beeping stops. Then he pushes the door open and we follow him inside.

Under his breath, Germ says, "Dude."

I don't know what I was expecting. Something so amazing it needs serious security, I guess. But it's just a dorm room. Blueprints cover the walls. Huge diagrams. Can't tell what they're of. Cars? Computers? A bed crouches low to the floor against the far wall. Above it hangs a framed picture of a blue phone booth. A long countertop with a built-in desk runs along the opposite side. Computer books and gaming manuals crowd the shelves above. On the desk sits a fishbowl. Everything is sleek and smooth and clean. Maybe the guy is just really paranoid someone's going to come in and muss up his sheets.

He opens a cabinet, pulls out a brown bag and tosses it to Germ. Then he moves his goggles up onto his forehead and rubs his eyes. "Two uniforms, as requested." He sees me staring at him, so I study a blueprint on the wall instead. The words are in another language. Looks like it's for some kind of safe.

"I don't know how you do it," Germ says. M holds out his hands like it's no big deal.

Walking over to the desk, I try to get a good look at M before leaning over the fishbowl. Beside it is a photo of a girl with braids. It's signed MISSY, with a heart. The fish darts away when I tap the glass. I stare into the water as a memory plays out in my mind.

Sixth-grade gym class. He was the scrawniest of the scrawny kids. My buddies and I pounced on him in the locker room when he had his back turned. Kept one hand on his mouth to cover his squealing. Took his clothes and stuffed him in an empty locker. Outside there was a girl with braids. I'm guessing she was the one who ratted us out. I got suspended, but that didn't matter. It wasn't like I wanted to be at school anyway.

Warren something. Can't remember his last name. Not sure I ever knew it, actually.

I look at his face. There's something different about him here. He's still scrawny, but there's something sharp about his eyes. He's smart and he knows it. But it's not just brains and ego.

Guts.

This Warren's gutsy.

"Cool fish," I say, trying to keep my voice calm, even though my brain is tripping out. Why did we do that to him? I don't even remember whose idea it was. I never really thought about it again. Until now.

"That's Betty," he says. "I tell her all my secrets."

Okay. Not sure how to respond to that.

"What do we owe you?" Germ asks.

Warren—do I call him Warren or M?—crosses his arms. "Your help."

Germ and I exchange glances. "Doing what?" he asks.

"Changing the world."

25

EEVEE

A sound wakes me. I'm lying on the bed, my legs still dangling off the end. I don't remember falling asleep. My clothes are dusty and my mouth feels like I've been eating socks. The sound comes again, a sharp *bang* at my window. I stumble over and pull back the curtain.

There, standing in the grass, is Danny. He waves and motions for me to come down.

This feels like a Moment. A pivot point. I have a decision to make: stay where I am, or leap into the unknown.

I leap.

"I'll be right down," I say, holding up my hand, knowing he can't hear me.

My reflection in the mirror is a train wreck. Sleep lines. Mascara-smudged bags under my eyes. And I'm still wearing last night's clothes. Not good. I quickly change and wash my face before slipping on my flip-flops and tiptoeing downstairs.

Outside, the cold air shocks my lungs. Morning tinges the

horizon, but streetlights still cast pale circles on the sidewalk. My feet move quickly, silently, as my heart pounds in my ears. My eyes search the shadowed lawn. He can't be far. There's my window.

I see him leaning against a tree. He steps onto the sidewalk. My feet hesitate, then move faster until we're standing face to face.

"Hi." His hands are tucked into his pockets. His hair sticks up a bit and his eyes look tired, but he's smiling.

None of this feels real.

"Hi." Looking at him, I feel a sense of calm wrestling with my nervousness. "You found me."

"I found you."

A light blinks on in the dorm room window next to where we're standing. "Want to walk?"

"Yeah," he says, looking around. "Sure."

We stroll side by side down the sidewalk along McConnell Hall. He keeps his hands in his pockets, and I keep my arms wrapped around me, but we walk close to each other and our arms brush now and then.

"So, this is where you go to school?" he asks, his voice low.

"Yeah. Do you go here, too?"

"I wish." He stops suddenly and looks at me. His mouth opens like he's going to say something, but he closes it again.

"What?"

"Nothing," he says, still looking at me. "I just . . . remembered something."

"Where *do* you go to school?"

"Arcadia Tech." He says it like a question.

"Oh." It hadn't occurred to me that the Education Panels might have assigned him to a trade school.

When the sidewalk ends, we continue on into the grass. It's spongy, and bits of cold dew flick onto my toes. Eucalyptuses and cottonwoods surround us, their trunks so large two people together can't get their arms around them. I pick up a leaf and twirl the stem in my fingers. We walk slowly, like the sun isn't rising on a new day. Like we have all the time in the world.

"So, last night . . ." I let the thought trail off, hanging in the space between us.

"Last night," he says, filling that space by taking my hand.

"That was—"

"Amazing," he says at the same time I say, "Weird." We stop and look at each other.

"I mean . . ." I try to backpedal. "Totally amazing. But also . . . weird."

"Oh."

I shake my head. I'm doing this wrong. "No, I don't mean you. Seeing you again is great. But millions of people in Phoenix and we find each other in that crowd?" I count on my fingers. "Last night. Abbot's. The museum. Three random meetings. That's pretty weird, don't you think?"

"Museum?" His eyebrows furrow, then relax. "Oh. Right. Yeah, that's weird."

"You don't remember?"

He doesn't say anything, but his face is totally deer-in-the-headlights.

"Really?"

"I . . . It's just . . ." He closes his eyes and exhales. "It's complicated."

"Well, maybe this will jog your memory." I lean forward and kiss him, and it's every bit as good as the first time.

No.

It's better.

26

Danny

I jog across the lawn, still feeling her lips on mine, and find Germ sitting on a railing, waiting for me. He sees my face and rolls his eyes. "Come on, Casanova. Let's blow this Popsicle stand."

It takes us forever to get back to our side of town. Too bad we don't have our own driver. All we have is a lot of walking and the light-rail. Upside is, it gives us time to talk.

"So that was the first time you met M in person?"

"Yep." Germ shifts the bag on his shoulder. "First time you met him, too."

"Too bad the other Danny missed out."

Germ smirks. "He'll be pissed. We've been doing deals with M for years, but always through a third party. We never could get close to him. He's super secretive. Impossible to find unless he wants to be found."

We cross a street and walk into a park. Early-morning joggers and dog walkers pass by. "Wanna hear something crazy?"

It's a risk, but trusting Germ has only been a good thing so far. "I know him from my other life."

"Shut. *Up*." He turns around and walks backward to face me. "You're friends with Mastermind, but not *me*?"

"He's not much of a mastermind there. And I'm not friends with him. Probably safe to say he hates my guts."

"Why?"

I look out across the park so I don't have to look him in the eye. "I sort of . . . bullied him. Bad."

His mouth falls open, which makes me feel like crap. "If you did that here, you'd end up wearing concrete shoes in the harbor."

I try to imagine either version of Warren being some kind of Mafia lord. It's weird how things are the same here, but different. Like a game with all the right pieces but a different set of rules. "In my world, he's a scrawny nerd."

Germ laughs. "Well, here M's got connections up the wazoo. Mess with Mastermind and you can kiss your ass goodbye."

We leave the park and walk into a neighborhood. The sun is starting to rise, and the clouds don't seem as heavy. A leaf scoots by on the breeze. I stomp on it, then pick it up and twirl it by the stem. "You know what else is crazy?"

"You know *her*, too." He sees my face and laughs. "Not like it's some huge surprise. You guys couldn't keep your hands off each other. I figured there had to be some kind of history."

The thought of her arms around me short-circuits my brain. I clear my throat. "The weird part is, we're not together in my world. She sits next to me in English, but we never talk. Also, I think she's friends with M."

"Hang on." He stops. "The other Danny, my best friend, has a thing going with the governor's daughter *here,* and he doesn't even tell me?"

"Governor's daughter?"

"That's Eevee Solomon, Governor Solomon's daughter." He starts walking again. "She's totally swank, dude. Wonder what she sees in a punk like you."

I swing but he dodges, laughing. "Seriously, though. Good thing she was there. That raid was insane."

"Yeah, we were lucky." The question I'd wanted to ask him up on the mountain pops into my head. "Hey, what are Bounders?"

"Crazy people," he says. "Ultimate survivalists. They'd rather live down in the DMZ than under the government's rules."

"DMZ?"

He gawks at me, then shakes his head. "Let me guess. In your world, there's no war with Mexico."

"No," I say, wondering if he's pulling my leg. "Not since a really long time ago. Like, before we were a country."

"Well, here we have a truce and a demilitarized zone to enforce it. It's been like that forever. Forty years or something. Anyway, Bounders go live off the land out in the middle of nowhere." He moves his finger in a circle by his head. "Like I said, *loco.*"

"Why doesn't the government just go round them up?"

"And break the truce with Mexico? Too risky."

Seems like a lot of things in this world are risky. "Think we should sign on for M's plan?"

"We don't have much of a choice," Germ says. "Once you know something, you can't unknow it, you know? Besides, we owe him." He rattles the bag.

"And if we get caught?"

He shrugs. "We'll just call your girlfriend for help."

This time I swing and get him.

"Come on," he says, laughing. "We're gonna be late to school."

I stop home, thinking I'll just grab my stuff and go. Germ waits while I run inside. I'm barely through the front door, though, when I freeze in my tracks.

Mom sits on the loveseat in the front room, her cane resting against her leg, a piece of paper in her hand. She looks wiped out, like she's been up all night.

And that's when I realize. She has been up all night. She slept there. On the couch. I was out, and she sat here waiting for me.

That's what parents do.

She exhales, relief written all over her face, and uses her cane to push herself up.

"Mom—"

She hands me the paper and walks out of the room. The corners are curled from her working her worry out on them. Inside, in angry caps, is Dad's writing.

WHAT ARE YOU THINKING?

I refold the paper and pinch the crease tight between my thumb and finger. I wasn't thinking, of course. Why would I? No one's ever cared about what time I got home. No one's ever cared if I even *came* home.

I stick my head out the door, where Germ is waiting. "You better go on without me."

"Everything okay?"

"Yeah," I lie. "Just some stuff I need to take care of."

27

EEVEE

Thursday passes in a blur. I'm both tired and exhilarated, and all I can think about is seeing him again on Saturday, like we planned.

After we said goodbye, I went back to my room and dove into a new painting. My mind raced with ideas as my brush returned again and again to the canvas. I walked through most of the day with a paint smudge over my right eyebrow, and when someone brought it to my attention, I didn't even care.

After my last class, I hurry back to my room to work on it some more. Setting an alarm so I'm not late for evening open studio, I flip all of my paintings over to their outlaw sides and sit down in front of the easel.

So far the painting is varying shades of black, spackled on with the palette knife. It looks like an angry storm. Cool, but not quite the effect I'm hoping for. I load up a brush with blue and work to lighten the center of the dark. Instead of a storm, it begins to look more like night. I use gray and ocher to pull the hint of a face from the shadows, eyes closed, mouth open in a silent scream. Two hands with palms flat, one at either side of the unseen body. White highlights to sharpen the pain and contrast the dark. In the blackness you can almost see her body, but it's kind of like looking at a star—the more you look right at it, the less you can see. It's a pretty cool effect. I'm surprised I could pull it off. The work I've done imitating Klee's *Melancholic Child* must be helping. The details of the face are surprising. Dark hair and eyes. She looks a lot like me. The alarm sounds. Forty minutes have passed by in a blink. I set her aside to dry, clean up my brushes and head out.

The evening is cool, and the breeze skitters leaves along the sidewalks. Students hang out in the open areas around campus and lounge in the grass beneath the towering trees. Seeing them makes me think of Danny, the feeling of his hand in mine. I wish he were here.

The door of the Fine Arts Building is heavy and creaks open. Inside, I'm met with the roar of the furnaces in the glassblowing shop. I tie my cardigan around my waist and maneuver through the hallways. Snatches of opera mingle with student voices and far-off footfalls. Pavarotti this time. *Vincerò. Vincerò.*

When I open the studio door, reality hits me. Scraps of canvas cover the worktable in the far corner. My paintings are still ruined. Belford is further away than ever.

Vivian is set up at her canvas under the window, working on her jury paintings, no doubt. I ignore her, pulling on my apron and making my way over to the corner that's been cordoned off like a crime scene.

The pieces of *Confidante* are now labeled like puzzle pieces and stacked inside a clear plastic bag. I've found some bits of what I think is *Virtue,* and more that I'm pretty sure are *Reading by Candlelight,* but not enough to try to piece either back together. *Candlelight* is the easier of the two to find, given the bright yellow hues, so I start sifting through the pieces again, my back to the room.

It doesn't take long before I'm knee-deep in hopelessness.

Bosca must sense it. He appears at my left, one hand on his chin, shaking his head at the mess on the table. "Come," he says. "Take a break. Paint something new." He leads me away from the table toward an easel he's set up.

"But you said I should try to find—"

He walks to the supply closet and pulls out a fresh canvas. "Now I say paint. See what happens."

I sigh, frustrated yet relieved. Painting is what I love and what makes me feel like me, so yes, of course, please let me paint. But—

"There's no way I can get new work done in time for the jury," I say, pulling my brushes from the cubby.

He waves off my concern. "Just paint. See what happens." He walks over to Vivian.

It's a little canvas. Maybe that's his thinking: create some small paintings that are good enough to represent what I've learned in the last two years studying under him. I guess it's worth a shot.

As I stare into the whiteness of the canvas, I hear Warren's words: *You know what you should do? Paint mash-ups of art and science.* I see his hands moving in slo-mo like an implosion. My own hands move instinctively, adding paint to my palette, choosing the right brush.

"Good," Bosca says, looking over Vivian's work. A female voice comes on the radio, spreading an aria through the room. I push the sounds away and focus. Using the same strokes I did for the night portrait back in my room, I build up a base of grays and blues before loading my brush with magenta. I lean in close so that paint is all I see, and try to imagine the space between atoms, the ninety-nine percent nothingness of electron shells, and touching without really touching. The bright purple swirls through the murky background. The color is powerful. The effect is dizzying. My body sways with the motion of the brush.

"What is this?"

Antonio's voice breaks the spell. My brush stops midstroke, purple paint seeping up through the bristles.

"This is . . ." He waves his hand at the canvas. "This is not you. This is like child's painting."

I pull the brush back.

"I thought—" I look at the black globe on the ceiling, the Spectrum camera inside. I press the brush into the canvas and swish it around, smearing the colors, destroying what I created. "This is just . . . a base coat."

He shakes his head and walks off muttering, then halfway across the room stops and puts a finger in the air. "Ah!" He turns back, a smile on his face.

He points at Vivian. "You." And he points at me. "And you." He motions both of us over.

Vivian and I make uneasy eyes at each other as we walk from our opposite corners to the center. She gets there first and crosses her arms, an annoyed look on her face.

"I have brilliant idea." Bosca grins, his fingers entwined and resting at the top of his stomach. "You will be partners. Work together."

I gasp at the same time Vivian says, "What?" We launch into reasons against his "brilliant" idea, but Bosca holds up his hands to silence us.

"Who is in charge? Yes. Me. Vivian, you help her with subjects. Eevee, you help Vivian with technique. Go."

Neither of us moves until he shoos us away. "Go. Be brilliant."

Brilliant.

Vivian crosses her arms again and stands with one hip sticking out. "There's more light where I'm set up."

I roll my eyes. "Fine." I walk back over to my station, pack up my stuff and move to the other side of the room, dumping the art-science mash-up in the garbage and grabbing a new canvas along the way.

She scoots her easel over. The tension between us is thick. As I set up my stuff again, I glance at the table where I sorted through my ruined paintings. Even sifting through my despair would be better than this.

The light on this side of the room emphasizes how empty my canvas is. The idea of painting anything on it right now is about as appealing as going to the Governor's Gala with Chad. After fidgeting with my brushes for too long, I try to glance at Vivian's work. She's turned it so I can't see. "What are you working on?"

She takes so long to answer I think maybe she's going to ignore me. "The old house over on Lone Mountain."

I step around to look. She bristles like a porcupine.

Her painting is fine, actually. The manor house is set back in the trees, with a blue sky above. It's nice. She's added fine details around the door and the walk leading to it. The fox-gloves are pretty.

She sighs. "Bosca says it's missing something."

He's right. It's missing warmth. Emotional connection. Soul. If it were my painting, I know how I'd fix it, but do I tell her? Do I help her chances with the jury? My own defenses go up. "I think it's good."

She dabs more green into the trees. "Thanks. What are you going to paint?"

"No idea." I go back to my stool and stare at the canvas. "Any *brilliant* suggestions?"

She touches her brush to her palette and returns it to the canvas. "Nope."

I close my eyes and let my mind wander. Was the rave really only a few hours ago? I take a deep breath, imagining I'm breathing in the dusty night air. Imagining I'm weaving through a sea of cars, through a chain-link fence, through an archway of stone. Lights strobe behind my eyelids. Opera fades to a droning that begins soft but grows until all I hear is the beat all around me. My mind searches for him among the writhing bodies.

"What are you doing?"

My eyes fly open. Vivian is staring at me. "You're, like, dancing or something."

"Oh." My face feels hot. "Sorry."

"It's distracting."

"I said I was sorry." I move my stool away and try not to think about how stupid that must have looked. Focus, Eevee. What do I paint? The castle's rock towers? The lasers? The people dancing? A zing of panic rushes over me as images of the DPC guards storming into the courtyard flash through my mind. No, no, no. All of those things could trace me to last night. I need to find something else. Something safe, but not safe. Something that looks innocent, but isn't.

And then the answer is there. I don't even need to close my eyes to see it. I add new colors to my palette, choose a brush and get to work. My hands move with the same instinctive-ness they had when I painted the portrait of the girl emerging from the dark. Inside, I have the same feeling of confidence. It's like a voice whispering, *This is right.*

"Is that grass?"

My hand jolts back from the canvas and I almost jump down Vivian's throat, but instead I take a breath and answer, "Yes."

"Huh."

She broke my groove. "How's your house coming along? Do you want help?"

She doesn't answer, but I can tell from her face she hasn't figured out how to make the painting work. I set my palette down and stand beside her. She's been working since we got here, but the painting looks exactly the same. And it still has no soul.

Her shoulders droop.

"You know what you should try?" I glance over at Antonio. He's humming and painting away. "A kitten."

She looks at me with her eyebrows furrowed.

"I'm serious." I'm not serious. "Kittens are a symbol of everything that is right in the world. What's better than a kitten? The jury will love it." Maybe I'm laying it on too thick.

"Really?"

She looks intrigued. Maybe I'm laying it on just right.

"Think about it." I give her an enthusiastic, and completely fake, smile.

It isn't a total lie. If she thought about it, she'd realize putting a kitten in her painting would make it the equivalent of hotel art. Hesitantly, Vivian returns my smile.

"See?" Antonio's voice carries across the studio. "Working together is so much better!" He launches into a crazy rendition of *The Barber of Seville.* I sit back on my stool and pick up my brushes, ignoring the guilt inside.

When I leave the studio, the guilt still nags me. That was maybe the jerkiest thing I've ever done in my life. Even if she deserved it. I didn't get another look at her painting, so I don't know if she put a kitten in or not.

On my way back to my room, I stop to inspect the grass where Danny and I walked. I study how all the different shades of green create a seamless image. Kind of like a Seurat or a Monet. From a distance, it just looks green, but up close, there's a whole range of colors.

Satisfied, I cross the street toward my dorm. A girl stops me. "Are you Eevee?"

I've never seen her before. "Yes . . . ?"

She hands me a piece of paper and walks away. I watch her disappear around the corner before unfolding the note.

At least this time I know how to read it.

547uRd4y 2 mckINl3y 428

Warren's room must be in McKinley Hall, and apparently I'm meeting him there on Saturday. What's it going to be this time, a house party?

28

DANNY

Dad carries a dish from the kitchen counter to the table. He hasn't said a word since he got home from work. Mom hasn't said much either. I tried talking to her before I left late for school, but she never came out of her room. After school, she busied herself around the house, moving away from wherever I was. I walked into the living room, and as soon as I said "Mom," she closed her book and went to the kitchen. I followed her in there but she turned the faucet on full blast and rattled the dishes. When I tapped her on the shoulder, she shut the water off and left, saying, "I'm tired. We'll talk later."

This whole caring thing? It's hard.

"Help your mother," Dad says, setting the bowl of potatoes on a hot pad. I jump out of my seat and rush into the kitchen to carry whatever's left that needs carrying. Mom takes two glasses of milk. I grab the third and a plate of roasted chicken and follow her back to the table. Classical music from the stereo in the living room fills the silence between us.

They both rest their hands in their laps and bow their heads. Dad looks at me through his eyebrows and I snap my head down.

He clears his throat. "Protect and guide us as we make our way in this world."

Mom adds, "Amen." I mumble it, too, and watch them for the next move. We dish out food. Eat. And say nothing.

Just when the guilt's about to consume me, Dad slams his knife down. "I can't believe you did that to your mother."

"Parker."

"No, Rebecca. This needs to be said." He glares at me. "She waited for you all night. *All night.*"

I stare down at my hands.

"Where were you last night?" He waits. When I don't answer, he lays into me, careful to keep his voice just under the music. "How many times do we have to go through this? They are watching you, son. Watching everything you do. You think you can just waltz around this city doing whatever you want? You think they don't know?" He spits the words out in a whispered hiss. "All they need is one reason—just one—to come in here and take our lives apart. But that's not even the worst of it. The worst part is what you did to this woman right here." His anger falters as he points at Mom, his eyes still on me. She looks down at her lap. He inhales, nostrils flared. "How dare you treat her with such disrespect."

When Brent is mad, he gets this look in his eyes that says, *If I could crush you, I would.* The look in Dad's—and Mom's—isn't like that, though. Angry? Yes. But also worried. And relieved. It kills me. I know how to fight, but this? I don't know how to react.

What if I just tell them everything? I think it through, plan it out in my head. *I'm not your son. I'm not who you think I am.*

Dad throws his hands up, exasperated. "It's like I don't know you anymore."

"I'm not—" They wait for me to continue. I can't do it. What if I tell them and they totally reject me? "I'm not going to do that to you guys again."

Mom nods. Dad gives me a long, hard look, then says, "Thank you," and picks up his fork and knife.

29

EEVEE

When Jonas picks me up Friday afternoon, neither of us says anything. Neither acknowledges what happened Wednesday night. But the weight of it sits between us. Only once do I catch him looking at me in the rearview. I'm sure he feels it, too.

We arrive late, which is a surprise. Usually, he drops me off so early I sit around with nothing to do. This time, though, we arrive just as the event is starting. I rush over to the grocery store entrance. Richard greets me with an exasperated sigh and points to where I should stand. Mom welcomes me with an arm around my shoulder. It's the first time I've seen her since our big blowout. She acts like all is forgiven, but maybe that's just because people are watching.

Dad, wearing a proud politician smile, stands next to Dr. McAllister. Behind them is a sign that reads STAND UP TO TERROR. A small crowd has gathered. It's all really casual. One of Dad's "man on the street" deals. Moms juggle babies and grocery bags, waiting for the show to start. A toddler who's had enough begins to cry.

"My baby cries when I give speeches, too," Dad says, giving me a wink. The audience laughs. The mom shushes the child.

"Thanks for coming out today, everyone." Dad holds his hands out as he speaks. "We're excited to announce an amazing development in our fight to stand up to terror: mobile Skylar scanners. How many of you saw the press conference Dr. McAllister and I held at DART last weekend?"

A lot of hands go up.

"Good, good," Dad says. "For those of you who didn't, or aren't familiar with Skylar, I'd like to have Dr. McAllister take a moment to explain how it works. Dr. McAllister?" Dad leads the audience in applause. Dr. McAllister moves to center stage.

"Skylar is the latest technological advancement in providing a blanket of protection over our city."

I watch the faces in the audience as Dr. McAllister explains how the system works. Many people smile, knowing they're on live TV. Here and there I see signs of unease, scrunched eyebrows or nervous glances at others, but for the most part, the reaction is no reaction.

"Looks like there are a lot of parents out here today," Dad says, taking his spot again next to Dr. McAllister. "Tell me, Mac, can I use Skylar to keep track of my daughter when she sneaks out?"

My mouth drops open. The audience chuckles. Dad squeezes me around the shoulders and kisses the top of my head. "Just kidding, honey."

I try to laugh it off, but I feel dizzy. How far does Skylar reach? My red *X* is a yellow dot. I never even thought about that. Does Dad know where I went Wednesday night? My hands start to fidget. Mom grabs one and holds it tight. I need to keep it together.

"Well," Dr. McAllister says, "the system isn't really intended for that use. . . ."

"I know, I know," Dad says. "But it will be good for tracking down bad guys, will it not?"

"Yes," Dr. McAllister says. "In fact . . ." He continues answering questions about the purpose of the system, how it will be used to track down terrorists, how the more Knowns there are, the easier it will be to identify Unknowns. In my mind I see the yellow circles moving on the Skylar grid. I wish I were still Unknown.

When they're done, the audience claps. Dad and Dr. McAllister step aside.

"Think they'll sign up?" Dr. McAllister asks when his back is to the crowd.

Dad keeps his voice low. "They better."

Richard instructs everyone to form a line. Some people line up in front of him, but most don't. Most walk into the store or out to the parking lot to their waiting cars. Dad watches them walking away. He doesn't look happy.

30

Danny

Friday after school, we drop off our backpacks, bag our paint supplies and head for the harbor to cause mayhem.

Well, maybe not *mayhem*. But that's kind of how it feels. Like when I'd be out all night with the guys back home, tearing up the town. I watch my reflection in the shopwindows, my ratty jeans and shades. Bag slung over my shoulder. Germ said the other Danny is confident. Well, here I am. What would Eevee think if she saw me? Maybe I'll try it out when I see her tomorrow. Germ looks pretty badass, too, strutting along, carrying the other bag.

It's kind of a lie, though. I keep thinking about the look on Mom's face when I walked in the door yesterday morning. The disappointment on Dad's when he came home from work. The promise I made not to screw up again. All that takes the edge off my appetite for trouble. Back home, the things I did only affected me. I can't be selfish like that here. My actions impact others now, for good and bad.

"We gotta be back before curfew." As soon as I say it, the veneer of badassery falls away. Probably better to just be myself with Eevee. Well, as much as possible, anyway.

"No problem," Germ says. "I got chewed out, too. Dad thinks I'm gonna wind up on the SPL." When I don't respond, he looks at me. "Sorry. The suspicious persons list."

A patrol car approaches, and we become unusually engrossed in the fine print of a sign in a shopwindow.

"Why'd you guys get involved with RD in the first place?"

Germ watches the car pass in the window reflection. "Paint's impossible to get. Those cans in your bag? That's our thank-you from RD."

"Isn't that kind of a big risk just for paint?"

He doesn't say anything, which makes me wonder if what I said ticked him off. I'm about to apologize when he says, "There's nothing like blazing the side of a building to show them they don't own us. That's worth it. To me, at least."

Can't argue with that.

We continue down the sidewalk. Seagulls squawk overhead, and the stink of fish guts and seaweed mixes with the saltwater air. When we get near the harbor, we turn down an alley and emerge at the back of our first target: a coffee shop with oceanfront seating.

"Here we go." Germ pulls two city utility worker coats and two hard hats from his bag. I pull a tarp and duct tape from mine. We put the coats on—his is way too large—and laugh at how stupid we look. I shake my head. "I can't believe we're doing this."

"I can." He grins, sticking out his hand in a way I haven't

seen before. When I put out my hand, he walks me through what must be his and Danny's secret shake: regular shake, bro shake, shoulder bump, fist bump.

Two scruffy teens walk into an alley. Two utility workers walk out. They hang a blue tarp to secure their work area and get busy. All in full view of Spectrum cameras.

And no one notices.

Two hours later, we've hit the coffee shop, a bookstore, a clothing store, a low wall in front of an apartment complex, the concrete moorings by the pier, and a billboard. The billboard was the toughest. Germ doesn't like heights. I don't like getting caught. But we did it, and now it's there for the world to see.

Doesn't seem like much, to be honest. Just words and pictures sprayed on brick, concrete, metal. But it's better than saying nothing at all.

Our bags stashed behind a Dumpster, we hang a right and cross a busy street along the harbor. It's getting late and we're taking a risk, but we circle back one more time to admire our work. I keep my baseball cap low over my eyes. Germ has his hood up. We walk along the waterfront. Waves slosh against the seawall. Seagulls stand like statues on the wooden pylons. I inhale as deeply as I can—I'll never get used to the smell of the ocean—and cough. A tightness in my chest.

"You okay?"

"Yeah." I clear my throat. The tightness fades. "Hope I'm not coming down with something."

Germ nudges me with his elbow and we slow down. A woman stands in front of our painting of the bar-code-head guy with hands covering his mouth. She's small and her back is hunched. She looks at the face on the wall. Only her gray curls move in the wind. We walk past her and stop under a tree, out of sight of the cameras. After what seems like a long time, the woman glances around. She fishes through her bags, pulls out her phone and snaps a picture. Then she picks up the bags and walks off down the road.

31

EEVEE

After days on end of gray clouds, sunshine filters through the trees, dappling the grass with patches of light. An ant crawls onto the blanket and I brush it away. Rabbits and birds skitter in the bushes on the other side of the school fence. It's a perfect day for a picnic. I smooth my skirt over my legs and check the time again. Maybe he changed his mind.

I touch the tip of my brush to the water and the blue tint spreads like liquid smoke. Then I wash the color across the paper, creating a cerulean sky before blending it down to a phthalo sea. With emerald I add grass, dabbing in layers of viridian and ocher for shadows and light. I'm just about to paint the sunset when a voice behind me says, "Hi."

I look up. The sun winks through the trees, fracturing my view of Danny with flares of light. The effect is dazzling. My eyes etch the image onto my brain so I can sketch it later.

"Did you make that?" He crouches down. "It's awesome."

It takes me too long to respond. I can't stop looking at his face. "What? Oh. Yes. Do you want it?"

He looks good. Really good. Ratty jeans. Rolled-up sleeves.

"That belongs in a museum or something."

"No. This is just me goofing around. It still needs to dry, but when it's done, you can have it."

"Thanks." He joins me on the blanket. "Sorry I'm late. Took the wrong train and got lost."

"I thought maybe you'd changed your mind."

"No way. I'd have been here early if I wasn't such a noob about the light-rail."

I blow on the watercolor and set it aside to dry. "Want to hear a secret? I've never ridden it. It scares me."

"Scares *you*? You don't seem like the kind of girl who scares easy."

"Oh yeah? And just what kind of girl *do* I seem like?"

He studies my face. "Not sure yet."

The way he's looking at me makes my hands fidget. "Hungry?" I open the basket to give them something to do. "I nabbed some muffins from the breakfast line. Is blueberry okay?"

"Perfect. Oh, hang on. I forgot." He reaches into his back pocket, then takes my hand. "This is for you."

In my palm is a smooth black stone. "What's this?"

"Just something I picked up from that castle place the other night. I wanted something to remember it by. Thought you might, too."

"Thank you."

He clears his throat. "So, what have you been up to?"

I reach into the basket and present a muffin to him with a silly flourish, then grab a second for me. Inside, I'm trying to figure out how to answer his question. Finally, I settle on, "Painting. You?"

He takes a bite and thinks, too, before answering. "Same."

Totally not what I expected. "You paint? Like, what, water-colors? Oils?"

"Um . . . spray?"

I stop midbite. "As in, graffiti?"

He pops the rest of the muffin into his mouth and rests back on his elbows, smiling as he chews.

"That's kind of illegal, you know."

He shrugs. Just like he did at the museum.

"I could totally turn you in."

"Yeah, but you won't." He picks up the watercolor.

"How do you know?"

"You don't seem like the kind of girl who'd do that." He looks at the painting. "Tell me about this."

I finish the last bite and brush off my hands. "What's to tell? It's the ocean."

"Why the ocean?"

I think about it for a second. "Because it makes me feel free."

"Have you been out on it?" He sets the painting down and leans back again on his elbows.

I scoot the picnic items over and lean back beside him. "Lots of times. Mostly for boring political stuff. Have you?"

"Nah. Boring political stuff's not really my thing."

I bump him with my shoulder. "The ocean, silly."

He smirks. "No. I was supposed to go last weekend but the harbor was closed."

"Last weekend everything was closed."

"Except the grocery store." He looks over at me. "Good

thing, huh?" He lies back on the blanket and puts his hands under his head.

It's been gray for so long. The sun shimmering through the trees is gorgeous. Reminds me of the leaves in *Confidante*. I sigh. "Do you ever wish you could go somewhere else?"

He brushes my hair away from my shoulder. When I look over at him, his face is intense. "Where would you go?"

I lie back next to him and fold my hands across my stomach. "Anywhere not here."

His hand reaches over and finds mine. When he speaks, his voice is quiet. "I used to feel that way."

32

Danny

I want to tell her so bad.

That I'm from somewhere else—and now that I'm here, I never want to leave.

Her hand is soft in mine. I listen as she talks about her life, and answer as much as I can when she asks about mine. The sun shines on us through the trees and everything feels perfect.

But short. The seconds tick down. Pretty soon I'll have to go meet with Warren and Germ.

She turns over so she's lying on her stomach, propped up on her elbows. "Do you dance?"

The question throws me. "I try not to."

"Let me rephrase that. What I *actually* mean is . . . would you like to go to a dance with me?"

"Like a school dance?" I make a face.

She makes a face, too. "Worse. Governor's Gala. I have to go and it's kind of expected I'll bring a date. My parents want me to go with this intern guy, but . . ." She rolls her eyes. "Please say yes."

What in the world is a governor's gala? Ladies in pouffy dresses and powdered wigs? I can't imagine myself in the middle of that crowd, but the way she's looking at me, I give in. "Okay."

"Really?" First she looks surprised. Then relieved. "Thank you."

"Thank *you*. Last time a girl asked me to a dance was . . . let me think . . . never."

"I find that hard to believe."

She has no idea.

We're both quiet, looking at each other. Wish we could stay like this all day. All day? Wish we could stay like this forever.

She leans in and whispers, "Why haven't you kissed me yet?"

A smile plays at her lips. I give her a daring look in return. "Why haven't you kissed *me* yet?"

We're so close, eye to eye, both waiting to see who'll make the first move.

And then there's harp music.

She startles and reaches for her phone. "I'm sorry. I have to go. There's this thing . . ."

"It's okay." I sit up, fix the back of my hair. "I actually have to get going, too."

She gathers up the picnic items. "When do I get to see you again?"

As I help her, an idea pops into my head. "Monday?"

"Not tomorrow?"

I consider it, but not knowing what Warren has planned, it's best to leave the day open. "Sorry."

She looks disappointed. I stop her hands and look her in the eye, trying to somehow make her understand all the things that are too difficult to say. Then I lean in and kiss her quickly because the clock is ticking and I'm bad at goodbyes.

33

EEVEE

It kills me that our picnic ended so quickly—why is our timing always so off?—but the sun is shining and his kisses are amazing and somehow it feels like everything is going to be okay.

At two o'clock, I knock on Warren's door. There's a series of *beeps* followed by a *click*. The handle turns and a begoggled face peers at me through the opening.

"Ha!" I grin. "Figured it out easy this time."

He looks past me. "Were you followed?"

"What?" I look down the hall. "No."

He opens the door and looks, too. Then stands back and lets me in. He's sporting his ankle pants again, and a serious case of bedhead.

His room is so clean it makes mine look like a hoarder's den. And I'm the only one here. Not sure what I expected, but it wasn't this. "I, uh . . . What exactly did you invite me here for?"

He lifts the blinds to peer out the window. "Just a little get-together with friends."

So there will be others. "Like, a study session? Or another dance party?"

He makes a slicing motion across his throat, holds a finger to his lips and points at the ceiling.

I look up. The ceiling is listening? "You're kind of starting to freak—"

Two knocks sound at the door, followed by a pause, followed by a single knock. Warren holds his hands out: *See?*

He opens the door and there's Danny. When he sees me, his jaw drops. So does mine.

"Funny meeting you here." He hugs me. Over his shoulder I see his friend Germ. Warren locks the door and punches buttons on a keypad on the wall. A ladder of lasers shoots from one side of the door to the other. Whoa.

So this isn't a study session. And it definitely isn't a dance party either.

Warren reaches under a cabinet and slides out what looks like a control panel. He presses buttons and there's a humming sound. It's so low, though, I don't hear it so much as feel it raising the hair on my arms.

"That's better," he says. He pushes his goggles up onto his forehead. "Dampening field." He says it like it's obvious and not at all weird. "Interferes with recording devices, scrambles imaging. You know." He pulls a chair out from the desk and holds on to the back with both hands. "Before we can get started, Eevee needs to decide if she's on board."

"For what?" I look at Danny. He gives me a small nod.

"The team," Warren says.

"You guys are a team now? Are we talking baseball or . . ." My nervous laughter is swallowed up in the dampening field. "You guys are serious."

Warren's eyes stay intent on mine.

"She's fine," Danny says. "Give her a break."

"Not until she agrees."

Agrees to what? The way the three of them are looking at me, I feel like bolting for the door, but this is Warren we're talking about. He's cool, right? And Danny is Danny. Still . . . "What if I say yes and later change my mind?"

"You won't," Danny says.

"How do you know?"

He shrugs. "I just do."

My stomach churns with the same helpless feeling I had in the bunker. This is another Moment. Once again I'm standing on the edge and it's time to decide whether or not I'm going to—

"Yes." I inhale sharply. "I'm in."

"Excellent!" Warren walks back over to the control panel and presses a button. The lights under the cabinets dim. Flatscreen monitors descend from the shelves. A projected keyboard appears on the desk. The fishbowl glows blue.

"Wha—?" My hands hang limp at my sides. "What's all this? Who *are* you?"

Warren doesn't answer, but Germ leans over and whispers, "Mastermind."

"Master . . . ?"

Warren moves across the room with precision. His fingers

type on the keyboard, and the monitors flash to life. One shows a map; another runs a display of coordinates. A third has only a blinking cursor, waiting for a command.

"What does the fishbowl do?" Germ asks.

"Oh, that's just because it looks cool."

"Hang on," I say, walking over to look at the monitors. "Isn't that Skylar?"

"Ding ding ding," Warren says, his fingers on the projected keys. "We have a winner."

I watch yellow dots roam the grid. "Is it live?"

"Not yet. They've run two successful tests, last Friday and again on Wednesday. A third is scheduled for Monday. Maybe it'll be dead by then."

"Dead? But you helped build it."

"Yep." He taps the desk where the ENTER button shines. "And now I'm going to take it down."

34

DANNY

Warren is brilliant. Weird. But brilliant.

By the end of the meeting, we really were a team. Four kids with a harebrained plan to change the world. Or at least shake it up.

Warren built these computer chips designed to disrupt the security network. We call them M chips. M for Mastermind, since he created them. Or mayhem, because that's what they'll cause. Or maybe even mercy, because that's what we'll beg for if we get caught.

He explained how they work. It's pretty technical and I'm not sure any of us really get it, but it sounds cool. Skylar piggy-backs on the Spectrum system, same network and hardware. He created a virus that will worm its way through and leave a path of destruction—*if* it can travel the system without being detected. That's where the chips come in. They carry a code that will override any alerts or error messages. It'll look like smooth sailing on the monitor even as the guts of the whole thing are being chewed up and spit out.

"Simple," Warren said, "but elegant."

Before we left, he gave us five each, to cover fifteen stations across Phoenix.

"The tricky part," he said, "will be planting the chips without getting caught."

Germ grinned. "We never get caught."

I look over at him now, holding on to the train railing, his face calm. I hope he's right. If this doesn't work and Skylar goes live, there'll be no way to move undetected in the city. And apparently, if Skylar is successful here, they'll install it nationwide. What would it be like knowing you could be tracked everywhere you went? I can't even imagine. But it's not going to happen, because we're going to get the chips installed and Warren's virus will kill Skylar dead.

The doors close and the train lurches forward. Neither of us says anything. Outside, the station slips away and the city slides into view.

Germ and I decide to combine our tasks—stencils and M chips—and by Sunday afternoon we've covered three whole sections of the city: upper downtown, lower downtown and out east near our own stomping grounds. At one point we almost got caught hitting the gas station by the baseball stadium. Even though we were set up—tarp and everything— around the side of the building, this guy got out of his car to ask us directions. Our utility worker costumes must be pretty convincing. He had no clue he was talking to a couple of teenagers, or that there was a ticking time bomb painted on the wall with SKYLAR scrawled in red.

When we finished stenciling, we stashed away our gear,

grabbed the case Warren gave us and headed for the train. My heart was racing when we went through security, but not loud enough to tip them off, because here we are.

The box looks like a tin of breath mints. You can even open it and eat a few if you want, but the bottom slides off and there's a place carved out where the chip goes. Like something out of a spy movie.

I glance over at Germ. He catches my eye and smirks, then his face falls back to completely serious. When we're painting the stencils, we laugh and goof around. But this? This feels different. Bigger. Scarier.

The train pulls to a stop and we step off. The sun is just starting to sink behind the tallest high-rises downtown. We get our bearings, finding street names and location markers, trying not to draw attention to ourselves as we move down alleyways and across intersections. At the corner of Butler and Eighth, we stop.

There it is. The first way station.

Warren said we might encounter DART employees running diagnostics. Sure enough, there's a work vehicle parked by the relay station, and a guy is hooking up wires to some gadgetry.

So we decide to take a lesson from what happened at the gas station.

Germ pulls his phone out and walks right up to the guy, distracting him by asking for directions. He's so good at it. The two of them are tangled up in confusion in no time. Meanwhile, I sneak around back and find the control box. It's smaller than I expected. Even though Warren explained the steps, it takes me a second to figure out how to even open the thing. Finally, the panel slides across, revealing circuitry that looks like a minuscule city map. I don't know what any of it is, but that doesn't matter. I measure two fingers down, like Warren said, and count four chips over from the left. Pull the old chip out. Slip the new one in—hopefully fast enough that no alarms go off or blips show up on radar or whatever they do to monitor these things. I slide the cover back in place and slink away, still hearing Germ chatting with the DART guy.

We meet up at the next corner and walk back to the train in total silence. We board again, no problem, and settle in for the ride home.

Germ mutters, "I can't believe I actually offered him a mint." We stifle a laugh and do the tiniest fist bump. One down, nine to go. Hopefully, they'll all be that easy.

The movement of the train lulls me into a kind of trance. I watch downtown sail by and think of Eevee, the sunlight on her face, her hand in mine. "Ever feel like everything is so perfect you don't even want to breathe because you're afraid it'll go away?"

A smile breaks over Germ's face. He leans toward me and singsongs, "Danny's in love."

I push him away. "No, I'm not."

"Listen to yourself, dude. You weren't like this with what's-her-face."

"Which one?"

"Exactly."

When I push open my front door—minutes before curfew—I'm met with blaring classical music and the most amazing smell ever. Whatever Mom's making for dinner, I want it in my stomach *now*. I'm so hungry I could gnaw off my own arm. I find her and Dad in the kitchen.

"Oh!" She startles when she sees me. "There you are. Did you boys have a good time?"

"Yep. What's for dinner?" I flip on the oven light to see. "And why is the music so loud?"

"Lasagna." She doesn't answer the other question, but Dad goes to the stereo and turns it down enough that we don't have to yell.

"Who won the game?" Dad asks.

"The other guys."

"Again?" He pulls glasses from the cabinet. "That's too bad."

The oven timer goes off, and we help Mom move everything to the table. Dad says grace and we dig in, talking about our days and what we did. I have to lie, which makes me feel awful, but I remind myself that it's all for the good, and that takes away some of my guilt. Then I realize there's something I can talk to them about. Something real.

"Hey, Dad. Do you have a suit I can borrow?"

He looks at me like I have two heads. "A suit? What for?"

"I, uh . . . I got invited to a dance."

Mom's face lights up. "By who? Is it Tricia?"

"No." Tricia? Sheesh, Danny. How many girls are there? I shake my head. "Not Tricia. It's another girl. Her name is Eevee."

"Is it a school dance?" Dad asks.

"Um, it's a bigger deal than that, actually. It's the, uh . . . Governor's Gala?" I shrug. "Not really sure what that is."

Dad lowers his fork. "What?"

"Yeah, I met this girl at a—" I realize I can't tell them about the castle, but then I remember what Eevee said about the first time she and Danny met. "A museum exhibit. About a month ago. Remember?"

"Oh," Mom says, "when they lifted curfew?"

"Yeah." I try to read Dad's face while I talk. He doesn't look happy. "Uh, so I met her there, and she's an artist, and also the governor's daughter, and she—"

They both say, "What?" at the same time.

"I'm sorry, son," Dad says, "but I really don't think this is a good idea. That's not somewhere you belong."

I look at Mom. She opens her mouth, then closes it again and looks at Dad.

Are they kidding? For the last two days, I've been spray-painting antigovernment propaganda and conspiring to crash the city's surveillance system, and I'm not allowed to go to a *dance*?

"The thing is," I say, looking back and forth between them, "I like this girl. I mean, *really* like her. And she likes me, too. And that doesn't happen . . . you know . . . all the time. So, I don't care about politics or government or any of that. She asked me on a date and I want to go. Do you have a suit I can wear, or should I find one somewhere else?"

Dad puts his elbows on the table and rests his mouth against his folded hands. His eyes are stern. He's thinking hard. Finally, he shakes his head. "Fine." He sets his napkin on the table and pushes out his chair. "Just don't tell them anything about us," he says. "About our family, our friends. Nothing. Understand?"

"Yes, sir."

He looks at his watch and runs a hand through his hair. "I need to go."

"Go?" Mom asks, surprised. "Where?"

"Meeting."

"But what about curfew?"

"I know." Dad's voice is sharp. "But there's something I need to do." He sighs. "Sorry. I'll be back as soon as I can."

"Be careful."

"I will." He kisses her on the top of her head, touches me on the shoulder and leaves.

35

EEVEE

Monday morning, I can't sit still. I don't know if I should be excited, scared or both. Danny didn't say what he had planned, just that I should be ready for a surprise. Between that, my new position on Team Mastermind and Bosca's idea for me to fast-track paintings for the jury, I'm a mess.

And if I'm being completely honest with myself, I'm not all that sure the effort spent trying to impress the jury is even worth it. Do I really care about their approval? Do I still want to leave? My feelings aren't as black-and-white as they were. They've gone a sort of neutral gray.

I dip my brush in vibrant green and dab it onto the canvas, adding depth to a grassy lawn, not unlike the one here at school where I had a picnic with a particular boy. Then I slick a smaller brush through thinned-out dark green and pull the shadows through. When I'm satisfied the range of colors matches the picture in my mind, I load a medium brush with ocher to paint a leaf. This one isn't a cottonwood, though. It's a maple, because maple leaves are a symbol of love. How I know that, I have no idea, but now there is a maple leaf lying on the grass in my painting.

I step back and look at what I've created.

It's not bad. I'm not sure it's something worth showing to a jury, but I don't really care. I like it. It makes me happy.

"You are smiling." Antonio leaves his work to see what I'm up to. "That makes me smile."

Standing beside me, he looks at the painting, grunts and rubs his hand over his face. I can hear the scruff of his stubble. "Something here." He points to the lower half of the painting. "For balance." Then he grunts again and says, "Yes. This is good. More of this." With a final nod, he walks to his own easel. I step back from my painting to try to see it better. He's right, of course. Something is missing. I load a fresh brush with muted green and close my eyes, seeing it in my mind before saying it in paint.

Our footprints in the grass.

With the smaller brush I add in dimension, shadow, depth. Then I step back and, in my best—and quietest—Antonio impression, say, "Yes. This is good."

My phone rings and my palette drops to the floor with a crash. Antonio curses in Italian. I fumble for the phone and barely get it to my ear in time.

"Hello?" I wipe my hands on a rag, keeping the phone pinned between my ear and shoulder.

"Ready for an adventure?"

A million butterflies launch inside my rib cage. "Yes."

"At the corner of Sutton and Grand is a brick building. On the side is a box. Inside the box are your instructions."

"For what?"

I can hear the smile in his voice. "See you soon."

He hangs up, leaving me with my brain spinning. Sutton and Grand?

"Everything is okay?" Antonio asks.

"Yeah." I wipe the paint off my phone. "It's fine."

How am I going to get there? Call Jonas? I don't know what Danny has planned. Maybe Jonas isn't the best option. A taxi?

The light-rail.

You don't seem like the kind of girl who scares easy.

I close my eyes and take a deep breath. I'm going to actually take the train.

With trembling hands, I clean up my mess, put the finished painting in a cubby to dry and set off on an adventure.

It's rush hour and the platform is full of people. Some are dressed in suits. Others look like they slept on the streets last night. Posters trumpeting the ease of the new Skylar registration plaster the station walls. After passing through security, I weave through the crowd, trying to take up as little space as possible as I look for the ticket kiosk.

I have no idea what I'm doing. I should just give up and call Jonas.

"Do you need help?"

I turn toward the voice. A woman in a pantsuit with braided hair smiles at me. Her face is kind. "How do I get a ticket?"

"Come on." She walks with me over to the kiosk, which is only a few more feet down the platform, and helps me buy a fare card.

"Where are you going?" she asks as a train pulls up to the platform.

"Sutton and Grand."

She finds the nearest stop on the map. "You're going to want the green line. This one is blue. See it on the train? Green will come along soon. You want the seventh stop, okay? Lucky seven."

"Lucky seven." I smile. "Thank you."

"You're welcome." She boards the blue train and it's just me making myself small again.

Finally, a green-striped train arrives at the station and I shuffle on board with everyone else. It's already crowded when we get on, and I have to ride standing, holding on to a pole. This isn't what I expected at all. I thought it would feel like a regular train. Comfortable seats and refreshment carts. Instead, people I don't know who live lives very different from mine surround me. They all seem at ease, but I feel strange. Out of place. The doors close and everyone sways as the train moves forward. The man next to me wears spicy cologne. A little kid squawks at the other end of the car. A small black dome watches us from the ceiling. The city whooshes by, and my fingers grip the pole tightly as I count the stops.

One.

Two.

Three.

The train fills up as we get closer to downtown. Outside,

the buildings evolve from houses to small businesses to looming skyscrapers. As soon as the scenery starts to look familiar, I feel better. If something happened, I could walk from here.

At the sixth stop, I scoot closer to the doors.

At the seventh stop, I step off the train.

I did it.

A brick building stands at the corner of Sutton and Grand. The lower level is a print shop with windows painted in bright colors advertising the current specials. Those on the upper levels look like generic office windows. I step around the side to the alley between it and the Laundromat next door. On the wall is a gray box. Worried someone will think I'm tampering with the power, I look behind me. Is Danny watching? I glance up at the building's cameras. They're pointed out toward the sidewalk. With shaking hands, I pop open the latch on the box and the lid swings open. Inside is a rolled-up piece of paper, held in place by a smooth rock like the one he gave me at the picnic. I grab both, close the box and dart back to the street.

The note is written in all caps.

TWO BLOCKS EAST. ONE BLOCK SOUTH.
GATE ON RIGHT.

At least it isn't written in Warren code.

My hands tucked into my pockets, I cross at the light and

walk the two blocks. The clouds are back, and the skyscraper windows reflect the gray sky. I usually see all of this from a car, not walking around. It's strange to actually see people's faces.

Two blocks is Seventh Avenue. I take a right, passing a restaurant with a crowded patio. On my left, the baseball stadium rises like a giant over the street. I've been there a couple of times, when Dad threw out the opening pitch. But we always arrived by limo.

The next block down, things look a little sketchier. The buildings are older, and there aren't as many people around. Danny's note said there'd be a gate on the right, but all I see is a security officer. Maybe I should ask him.

As I get closer, the space between two buildings opens into a colorful courtyard. I hook my fingers through the chain-link fence and peer inside. Spray-painted artwork covers every inch of the walls. Is this real? It can't be legal. But there's a security guy right here, watching. It doesn't make sense.

I clear my throat and ask him, "Can I go in?" He looks at me with steely eyes and nods.

Even the concrete floor blooms with color. I watch my shoes step across flowers, robots, faces, words. It's amazing.

"You made it."

I know his voice before I even look up. Danny has on the same shirt he wore the night I met him at the museum. He gathers me into a hug. "Ready to paint?"

"What? No. No way."

"Come on." He shakes two cans and the marbles rattle and ping. "Give it a try."

"I do oils. Not graffiti."

"You do art." He hands me a can and kneels down to spray the ground, his shirt pulled up over his nose. I watch the lines connect into letters, and the letters turn into my name. He stands up and the shirt falls away from his face. "What kind of adventure is it if you're standing around watching?"

He's right.

I pull my shirt up over my nose, too, and step back, careful to avoid my shoes. The nozzle presses hard into my finger as I paint black letters connected to his blue, morphing the *E-E-V-E-E* into *D-A-N-N-Y*. His letters are blocky, angular. Mine are soft, rounded. When I finish the *Y*, I look up and see him smiling.

He walks over to the back wall and I follow. Together we go crazy, painting one picture after another, laughing as we rush back to the bin of paint cans by the entrance, grabbing different colors and chasing each other around the square. When we get too loud, the guard looks back at us and we settle down. Kind of.

Danny starts a line on one wall and I start one on the opposite side. We race each other, seeing who can get to the center first. My laughter echoes off the concrete and my line jags all over the place as I run, keeping an eye on him. At the corner, my shoulder smashes into the wall, but I keep going, my shoes clomping against the ground as I rush to meet him.

He stops short of the finish point and drops his arm to his side. I stop, too, inches from him. God, his eyes. I want to paint a sky that color blue.

His paint can clangs against the ground first. He steps toward me as I fall into him. Then his lips are on mine and the cameras are watching and for the first time in my life I don't care.

There's always that strange moment when you walk into your room with someone who's never been there before and it makes you kind of see it for the first time. The place is a mess. I think of Warren's neat-freak bunker and cringe. My bathrobe hangs from the back of my easel, and paint tubes are scattered everywhere. Pajamas didn't quite make it into the hamper either. I scoop them up with an apology, then pick a pillow off the floor and toss it back onto the loveseat.

"Don't worry about it," he says. He focuses on the artwork on the walls. "These are great. Did you paint them?"

"No, those are all prints." I take a deep breath. "But these are mine." I turn each one over to reveal my copycat outlaws on the reverse side. "Kind of."

"I know that one," he says, pointing at *Starry Night*. "Van Gogh, right? I've seen it before."

"You *have*?" I say, surprised. "Where? It's banned."

"I . . ." He looks at me, confused, then turns back to the paintings. "Don't remember."

I slide the Retrogressives book out from underneath my mattress and join him in front of my version of Klee's *Melancholic Child*. "See?" I point to the original in the book. "I still don't have the blending in the background right."

"Yeah, I was gonna mention that." He smirks and walks over to the canvas resting against the arm of the couch.

My fingers know their way to *Ma Jolie* without my even trying. "That's Picasso. I couldn't quite match the gray tones around—"

He puts a finger on my lips. "Why are you trashing your work?" He steps around me to the painting on the easel, and I follow. "That one's mine." I say it like an apology. I can't help it.

He looks at it closely. "I like it the best."

"You don't have to say that."

"I know." He turns to face me. My shoulders relax and my hands go calm. There's something fractured about him. Something beautiful and broken. When I look at him, it feels like everything will be okay. He leans in close, looking in my eyes, and whispers, "Why haven't I kissed you yet?"

"I don't know. Why haven't—"

He cuts me off, reaching for my face and tracing my jawline. The scent of spray paint lingers on his clothes and skin. The book drops from my hands.

There's no telling who kisses first.

36

DANNY

McGuffy's is packed by the time Germ arrives. It takes him a minute to find me at the two-seater in the far corner. He fills his cup with a mix of four different sodas and flops into his chair. Then he sits up straighter, staring at me with his eyes wide. A smile turns up one corner of his mouth. "Shut up."

"I didn't say anything."

"Shut *up*."

"What?" I lean back in my chair.

"I know that look."

"I don't know what you're talking about."

"You saw her." His voice gets louder. "But you didn't just *see* her, did you?"

"Why don't you shout about it," I say as cool as I can. "I don't think that guy over there heard you."

"Dude. It's so unfair." He pounds the table with his fist. "Every. Single. Time. Did you ask her if she has any cute friends?"

"Sorry." I shake my head. "Too busy."

"I bet you were." He raises his eyebrows and takes a swig of soda. "Well, maybe over in your world, all the girls dig me, huh? *Huh?*" He nods emphatically. "That's what I'm saying."

"You go on believing that."

"I will." He checks out who's sitting around us. "So, what do you think?" He tips his head toward the window. On the patio, a garbage can sports a spray-painted bloodshot eye. It isn't ours. "There's fresh paint all over town and we haven't lifted a finger."

I tap the bottom of my cup to knock the ice loose. "Looks like we struck a nerve."

"So let's keep going. Let's add more."

I keep my voice low. "Too risky. They'll be watching. I say we let whoever's doing the new stuff take over. Besides, we still have M chips to install."

"True." He sighs. "It's just . . . something's actually happening, man. I can feel it. I wanna be part of it."

"You are part of it, dummy. You *started* it." I chomp down the ice while he argues his case. Suddenly my chest gets that tight feeling. High-pitched ringing starts up in my ears. "Germ?" My voice sounds far away.

The ringing turns to static as cold floods through me. I feel my hands gripping the table, feel the floor beneath my feet, but my vision swirls black. I squeeze my eyes shut, and when I open them again, I'm lying on my back. My body buzzes. I see a white ceiling, a poster of Einstein, a drawing of squares on a white piece of paper.

Then, in the buzzing, I feel him—the other Danny—reaching across, pushing through me. I slip farther toward the other side. The bedroom comes into focus. I can taste the air, sense the tightness of my old body.

No.

I focus on the sandwich shop. Germ's voice. My fingers digging into the wood of the table. I stomp my feet on the floor. The bedroom shifts, then dims, and suddenly I'm back. The cold slips away, replaced by a thousand ants crawling under my skin. Breathless, I slide down into the chair, my hands still clutching the table's edge. Germ stares at me, his mouth hanging open.

"What the hell was that?"

I look at my hands. The buzzing in my chest fades. "I don't know."

But I do know.

It was him, on the other side. The other Danny, trying to get through. "Come on," I say, noticing people staring. "Let's get out of here."

Outside the shop, Germ asks, "Has it happened before?"

I look him in the eye and nod. "Once. At the castle."

"Shit." He runs a hand over his face. "It was like you were having a seizure or something."

"It wasn't a seizure." I close my eyes and steady my breathing. "It was the same thing as when I jumped here."

"The Swirling Vortex . . . ?"

"Of Doom," I finish, my voice grim. "Today is Monday, right?"

"Yeah. Why?"

I sigh, remembering what Warren said. *Friday and again on Wednesday. A third is scheduled for Monday.* Every day they've tested the system, I've had an episode, including the day I first got here. "This is going to sound crazy," I say, "but I think it has to do with Skylar."

37

EEVEE

After, I sit on the floor, swirling a brush in a mason jar. The water is murky brown and really should be changed, but I don't want to leave the painting that's emerging on the paper in front of me. I'm so close to capturing the sun-fractured look he had at the picnic. The bright green of the trees surrounds his head like an aura. A flare of white obstructs his face. I touch the tip of the brush to the sky, feathering the blue like clouds.

There's a knock at the door. My first thought is, *He's back.*

I set the paintbrush down, tiptoe through the watercolor mess and open the door.

But it isn't him.

It's *her.*

"I can't believe I trusted you." Vivian's eyes are like daggers. Her hands grip her manor house painting. "A *kitten?* Bosća said it ruined my—" She stops short, her mouth hanging open, and we both realize what she's seeing.

My walls, covered in outlawed artwork.

Oh no.

I'm doomed.

Her eyes move from the artwork back to my face. She smiles. It's the same look she had the night she caught me at the museum.

"Vivian." I keep my voice low. I'm sure my neighbors can hear us. And the hallway camera is always watching. "*Please.* Let's talk about this."

"You want to talk? Fine." She pushes past me, handing me her painting. I close the door and watch her move around my room, examine each canvas. Every time she looks at one, it feels like a violation. She spends a long time peering down at the just-begun watercolor on the floor. Then, when she's done scrutinizing the contents of my soul, she strolls back over to me. Her face is cold, triumphant. "A most *enlightening* collection. I'm sure people would be really interested in knowing about it. Bosca. The Art Guild. The Education Panels. Your dad's constituents. Should I keep going?"

"*Please,* Vivian," I whisper. "It doesn't have to be like this. Remember how we used to be, before our dads and all the political stuff? Let's just forget about this and go back to being friends."

She laughs. "Sorry. I have no desire to be friends with a freak."

I swallow my anger and set the kitten painting aside. I'm in no position to argue. "I'll do anything you want."

"Anything?"

I nod.

She knows she's beaten me. "Okay. I'll keep your ugly secret safe. But in return, you have to finish my paintings for Friday."

"But—"

"I'm not done." She crosses her arms. "If I don't get approval from the Art Guild, all bets are off. Whisper a word of our deal to anyone, and you'll be sorry."

"But there's no way to guarantee the guild—"

She shrugs and starts for the door.

"No. Wait." I close my eyes. "I'll do it."

Any plans—albeit unrealistic ones—I had for getting my own work ready for the jury are definitely out the window now. The time I have for planting M chips is in jeopardy, too. Stupid move, Eevee. You really blew it this time.

"Well, then," she says, clasping her hands. "Let's get started."

"Now?"

"No time to waste." Her smile is sweet. I'd like to rip it right off her face.

●

We work for two hours. We finish one painting. I'm exhausted, but still have so much to do.

When I'm sure she's gone, I change into ratty jeans and running shoes. Find the oldest shirt I own. Gather my hair up into a ponytail and pull it through the back of a baseball cap. With my shades on, I look nothing like myself. Which is good. I double-check that the M chips are inside my lipstick case and head out.

My first swap is located west of campus, two blocks north

of the Gateway light-rail station. Warren said for most of them we'd work in teams, but that this one should be easy enough to do on my own. DPC patrols aren't as heavy out here in the boonies.

Unlike this morning, I navigate the rail station like a pro. No need to ask questions or get help. My heart thumps a bit when I go through security, but the guard just shifts the contents of my bag and waves me forward. At the kiosk, I add a round-trip to my fare card, double-check my stop on the map and sit on a bench at the platform to wait. Behind me hangs a poster of a woman with blue eyes and a serious look on her face. Bold letters across the top read WE'RE IN THIS TOGETHER. And across the bottom: IT IS YOUR DUTY TO REPORT SUSPICIOUS ACTIVITY. Oh, the irony.

It's not yet rush hour. The station is nowhere near as busy as it was this morning. Just a couple of other people waiting. One stares at his phone. The other stares off into space. A janitor pushes a broom along the opposite platform. It makes a quiet swishing sound. Pigeons walk across the kiosk awning, heads bobbing with each step. I close my eyes and imagine Danny with me, the warmth of his skin, the taste of his lips. Try to find that feeling of peace. How has it only been a few days? I feel like he's always been a part of my life.

The rush of the approaching train startles me. I pull my cap lower on my forehead and choose a seat by the window. The doors close and the train eases away from the station.

Houses and neighborhoods whir by. The green blur of a park. The glinting windows of a busy shopping center. Everyday people doing everyday things.

At the first stop, a group of chatty young people board the train. Their faces are animated, their words hushed. My ears pick up *gutsy, security, caught*. I wonder what—or who—they're talking about. I move toward the doors so I'm ready to get off when the train stops, but as we approach the station, the car goes silent. Fingers point out the windows. Taking up the entire side of Sports 'n More is the face of a giant man. Painted in black and gray and white, it towers over the street. His eyes are piercing, and across his forehead are the striped lines of a bar code. Below him are the words WE ARE NOT NUMB—the E, R and S have already been power-washed away by two city employees. An armed DPC officer stands guard as they work.

A sick feeling overwhelms me. The train doors open, but my feet won't move. They close again and the train departs with me still on board.

38

Danny

We decide to talk to Warren, even if it means telling him my secret. If Skylar is somehow related to why I jumped here, then he's my best chance of figuring out why, and how to stop it.

So Tuesday morning, we walk to the rail station. Neither of us says much. Probably because there's too much to put into words: the M chips, our graffiti, the mystery graffiti, the Swirling Vortex of Doom. Or maybe it's that neither of us wants to admit that everything feels so huge and the odds of it all falling apart have suddenly skyrocketed. To top it all off, I can't help but wonder if Germ secretly hopes the other Danny will come back.

He nudges me with his elbow and nods at our FEAR = CONTROL painted on a newspaper stand. Beside it is someone else's design: a camera with an eye for a shutter and the words SMILE, THEY'RE WATCHING.

We wait for traffic to clear before crossing Central and heading toward the security check. Up the street, the sharp corner of the Phoenix Art Museum juts into the sky. That's where they first met. Images of Eevee flood my brain. I try to push away the thought that maybe she'd rather have the other Danny, too.

"You okay?" Germ asks.

"Yeah." I tuck my hands into my pockets.

During the SVOD, I saw a room. In that room was a sketch with a repeating pattern of squares. I saw that same drawing the morning I jumped here, in the notebook of the girl who sits next to me in English. I think that room belongs to the other Eevee. That had to be her I saw during the SVOD at the castle. Why would I see her, though, and be in her room? I don't even know her.

But the other Danny might.

"Whoa."

Germ grabs my arm. "Is it happening again?"

"No." I shake my head. "I was just thinking. What if the other Danny and the other Eevee get together? That would be—"

Germ's eyes go wide as the sound of an engine fills my ears. All at once, voices shout, hands grab. Germ's face twists to anger as I'm dragged backward into a van. A hood slips over my eyes. I hear the doors close, hear the engine rev, hear the tires squeal as we speed away.

My stomach churns, sick from the motion of the swaying van, but I don't dare puke with this hood over my head. The hard metal floor digs into my shoulder and hip. Every time I try to get up on my knees, the bouncing of the road tumbles me over again. Exhausted, I lie still instead, saving my strength for whatever's coming.

Finally, the van slows. Gravel crunches under the tires. Wherever we are, it's far from where Germ and I were. Did they get him, too?

The doors open. As they grab me, I try to make my body weigh more than it does. *You want to drag me, you're gonna drag dead weight.* The hood slips away and I see double doors guarded by a man with a gun. Screw this. I take the opposite tack: writhing like an angry cat. None of it matters, though. These guys are strong and they're good at what they do.

On the other side of the door the walls are bare. Pock-marks and cracks speckle the concrete floor passing a foot below my face. They lug me down a narrow hallway lined with closed doors. The third door on the left opens and I'm carried through, my feet kicking as two thugs make me stand, clamping my hands to my sides and forcing me upright.

In the center of the room, taking up most of the tiny space, is a pod. White and shiny, it looks like a clam with its shell open. Blue light ripples across water inside.

A young guy in scrubs approaches. He's shorter than me. "Hold still." When I spit in his face, he closes his eyes and clears his throat. "Thank you. Now hold still." He reaches up and sticks white electrode pads on my temples.

"The clothes," he says, motioning to the two guys before wiping his face with his sleeve.

Oh, hell no. I fight to push them away, kick out my legs, let my weight drag them down, but they wrestle me to the ground, and in a matter of seconds they've stripped me bare. Scrubs sticks two more pads on my chest, one on my side and one on my back. He presses what looks like putty into my ears and gives the goons a nod. They pull me across the cold floor to the pod and lift me like I weigh nothing. I land inside with a *sploosh* and the lid of the pod closes, swallowing me again in darkness.

39

EEVEE

Jonas takes a right, easing the car onto Central. The bell tower of San Xavier rises into the gray sky. Mom chatters away about all the latest news: Dad dealing with the special legislative session, and her own late nights planning the last-minute details of the gala, and isn't it nice to be able to take a break for some girl time, and how are the paintings coming along?

I lean forward to peer out the front window. The side of the Phoenix Art Museum rises like a ship out of the concrete. That's where it all started. That's where I first met him.

Jonas slams on the brakes. Mom yelps and does that thing where she flings her arm out to protect me, even though the seat belt holds me in place.

"Sorry," Jonas says, watching out the passenger window. "That van came out of nowhere."

"Well, be careful." Mom sits back and crosses her legs.

"Yes, ma'am." He inches the car forward, picking up speed after we're safely through the intersection.

"As I was saying," she says, smoothing her skirt, "after dress shopping we need to go to Everly's to finalize the floral arrangements. There's so much to do before the gala. It keeps me up at night wondering how it will all get done. But enough of me, honey. How is school?"

School? I haven't thought about school in days. I have no idea how school is. Did I miss a test? "Fine. Nothing new."

"And the Art Guild jury? Dad said you were trying to put your paintings back together."

I think of the box of scraps tucked in the cubby beneath mine at the studio. I squirreled away what was left of *Confidante* in my room, but I've pretty much given up on the rest. And now that I'm busy helping Vivian—the thought of her makes my stomach turn—fix her paintings, I haven't had time to do anything jury-worthy. "Doesn't look like that's going to work after all."

She puts her hand on my knee. "I know you're disappointed. But you can always try again next year." She's being kind, but we both know she's relieved. "Or maybe it's time to try your hand at something else."

Something like treason, Mom? Subversion? Lawlessness? How about fraud? Vivian and I have been giving that one a go. I smile innocently. "Maybe."

Mom sits in the mirrored dressing area at Diamond's, sipping cucumber water while I try on dresses picked out by our personal shopper. "Oh, that one's lovely. It's a good color for your skin tone."

I turn to examine the back of the dress in the mirror. "I

look like a waterfall. And these are hideous." I fiddle with the rhinestones on the front. "They scream, *Look at my boobs.*"

Mom waves a hand. "Fine. Next."

I step off the viewing platform and go back to the changing room. The next dress is a deep red with spaghetti straps. Definitely more my style. I slip the waterfall off and put it back on the hanger.

"So, tell me about this boy," Mom says, her voice so loud I'm sure she has the attention of the entire store.

"He's from school," I say, pulling the dress over my head. It's getting so easy to lie.

"Is he an artist?"

"Yes." Only half a lie this time. I reach around to zip up the back, then smooth my hands down the front. This one's nice. I like it.

"Is he part of the fine arts studio?"

"No." It kind of reminds me of the dress I wore the night of Bosca's exhibit. It's a deeper red, though, and has a chiffon overlay. Maybe it will make him think of the night we first met. I lean toward the mirror, pretending I'm leaning toward him.

"Well, I guess not everyone is talented enough to make it in, right?"

I roll my eyes. "He's talented, Mom."

"Oh, I have no doubt," she says, still too loudly. "You've always had an eye for the talented ones. You take after me that way. . . ." She chatters on, winding her monologue around to how she met Dad at school and how talented *he* was, but not in art; no, he had ideas, vision, a passion for steering people toward their potential. I've heard the story so many times I know it by heart. He sat behind her in political science class. Every day from the day they met he asked her to go out with him, and every day she said no—"Always play hard to get, honey"—until *finally* she gave in and he took her to the homecoming dance. "We've had our ups and downs," she says, and I mouth along as she finishes with, "but we make a pretty good team."

I pull my hair up to see how it looks. With some sparkly earrings, this will do nicely. I open the door and walk to the platform. Mom clasps her hands in front of her. "Oh, Eve."

"Yeah?" I say, twirling to see every side in the mirrors.

"Your father won't like the straps, though. Too much skin."

"Don't care." I pull my hair up again to show her.

"You look beautiful." She sounds like she's going to cry.

"It's not like I'm getting married," I say, letting my hair fall again. "It's just the gala."

"*Just* the gala?" She takes a sip of cucumber water. "It's going to be a night to remember."

40

Danny

Every cut, every scratch on my body stings, and the water tastes salty. Waves slap against the sides of the pod. My arms reach out as my feet search for the bottom. It isn't deep. The water is warm, though, and strange. When I stop struggling, it lifts me up. The stinging begins to numb. Soon I don't feel the water at all. I lie still, listening for any sound outside the pod, but all I can hear is my own breathing. I'm floating in darkness. Lost.

Lights blink on and I squint. Blue and purple colors splash across the domed ceiling. Despite the earplugs, I hear whispering through the water. A single voice—can't tell if it's male or female—starts low: "I feel safe and secure. No one wants to harm me."

A second chimes in, also low, echoing the first. "I feel safe and secure. No one wants to harm me." The voices weave together, a chorus of whispers overlapping, fading in and out with the colors. "Compliance is good. I relinquish control. I feel safe and secure. . . ."

The colors dazzle my eyes. Swirling in slow circles, they draw me in, pulling me closer. My eyes lose focus and my muscles go slack. The desire to fight slips away. The whispering voices calm my mind.

This is good. This is good.

Wait, where am I? I blink. The colors come into focus, then slip away again.

It doesn't matter. Nothing matters. This is good.

A sudden cold blooms across my chest. Every muscle contracts. My arms grasp for something to hold but there's only static in my ears, darkness in my eyes. As I fall, I feel the other Danny pressing through. I force my eyes open and see a warped image of the Rage poster above my bed at the foster house, the slashed screen on my window, the stop sign over the door. Through the static comes Brent's booming voice. The sound is raw, like feedback through a busted amp. Like the sharpening of knives. It feels like it'll shred me into pieces.

I can't go back there. I won't.

My legs kick as I fight the other Danny back. I force air into my frozen lungs, bite down and growl until the pain blooms colors back into my eyes. Blue and purple glow on a white domed ceiling. Waves slap against the walls of the pod. Whispers tell me I feel safe and secure, but now they're just words, just noise.

41

EEVEE

As Jonas drives to the Executive Tower, Mom chatters away about the guest list, the catering, the many things she still has to do. She's excited, and for good reason, I suppose. All is right in her world. I slip my phone out and check again for missed calls or messages, then, disappointed, put it away.

". . . don't you think, honey?"

"Huh?" I have no idea what she's going on about now. "Yeah. Totally." Sometimes it's better to just agree, whatever it is.

"I think so, too. I figure the more choices we give them, the better. Some people don't like mushrooms, you know."

Ah. She's circled around to the food again. I stare out the window, watching the buildings, cars, people. A pink-orange sky peeks out between the high-rises. I bet the sun setting over the water is gorgeous right now. Wish I could see it. With Danny. I check my phone again. Still no calls. Wherever he is, I hope he isn't cooped up somewhere listening to someone rattle on about mushrooms. I look across the car at Mom. Even in the darkening light, I can see she's beaming. This is her thing. She's in her element. She feels about this stuff the way I feel about art. Who am I to resent her for that?

"What?" she says, noticing me smiling at her.

"Thanks for taking me shopping."

"We had a nice time, didn't we?"

Our goodbye is short. Jonas pulls into the parking garage and leaves the car running at the curb while he gets the bags from the trunk. "See you soon, honey." Mom gives me an awkward hug across the backseat. I watch her gather her things and go inside.

By the time we're back on the road, the sun has set and night crouches over the city. Jonas steers the car through the last tangles of rush-hour traffic. I peer out at the lights shining down on businesses, neighborhoods. There's something anxious about them, something eager. Or maybe that's just me. My hands fidget, clicking the MUTE button on my phone off and on, off and on. When the freeway rises and the blacked-out site of the attack spreads to the south, I sink back into the seat, struck by the stark contrast. For some, the world is all glittering parties and fun. For others, it's dark and full of fear. For me, somehow, it's both.

42

Danny

First they throw me my clothes and watch me get dressed. Then they throw the hood back over my head and load me into the van. I play along, sitting motionless with my back against the metal side. Whatever that was, it was meant to make me obey. It was effective, too. Before the other Danny broke through, I could feel it taking hold. Better pretend it worked or they'll do it again—or worse—until I really am their monkey.

The van jolts forward. I try to figure out where we are by the direction of turns, the number of stops, the sounds outside. It's impossible, though. I don't know the city well enough. I count two rights, a left and another before losing track.

Finally, we stop. The doors open. In one swift movement, they pull off the hood and push me out. I crash onto the side-walk. The tires smoke as the van pulls away.

I look around. The sky is dark. The street is empty. It must be after curfew. I've been gone all day. On the corner is the gas station where Dad filled up the truck before we took the boat out. Which means home is—I turn around—this way.

When I open the door, Mom, Dad and Germ rush at me. Mom's eyes are red from crying. They bombard me with questions, with hugs. I hold out my hands, stumble to the nearest chair and collapse.

I'm home. I'm safe.

"I ran over here right after," Germ says, talking fast. "Your dad's been making calls all day, but—"

Dad rests a hand on Germ's shoulder. Mom takes him by the elbow and moves him back so Dad has room to crouch in front of me. He peers into my eyes. "How are you, son?"

How am I? "Waterlogged." I take a deep, shuddering breath. "I'm fine. Everything's fine." His eyes widen, and I realize I sound like the whispering voices. "No, not fine. I mean, I'm just banged up a bit."

Dad stands and nods at Mom. "Hydro."

She covers her mouth. Germ puts his arm around her and looks at me like I'm infected with some kind of virus. I push myself up from the chair. "It didn't work, guys. Whatever it was, I'm fine."

They don't believe me.

I get in Germ's face to make him pay attention. "*Something happened* during that . . . procedure. When the voices started, it was like my brain switched off and *went somewhere else.*"

He gives me a questioning look, then mouths, *Really?* I nod. He understands.

Dad exhales, looking up at the ceiling, his hands on his hips. The light casts harsh shadows across his face. "This is my fault."

"What?" Germ and I say at the same time.

"They're warning me," he says. "Or punishing me."

Mom walks to the stereo and turns on classical, loud. When she returns, the four of us stand in an awkward circle beneath the spinning blades of the ceiling fan.

"There's this group," he says, his voice just under the music. "They approached me about getting involved with . . ." He pinches the bridge of his nose. "Well, let's just be real here. They're against the government."

Germ and I exchange looks. "You mean like Red December?" I ask.

"No. Not that bad. But . . ." He shakes his head. "It started with just meetings. Gripe sessions, venting, that kind of thing. But then it changed. Less complaining, more action, and I agreed to do what I could to delay the installation of the Skylar transmitters."

That's his job?

"And you know, it worked. For a while. The last bit of hardware was installed on Monday, two whole months late. The guys, though, they came up with a new plan. Something I just couldn't get behind. When I suggested a different idea, they kicked me out. Thought I was a government spy." He shakes his head, a wry smile on his face. "Me. A spy." Then he puts his hand on my shoulder, "I'm sure this was their way of keeping me quiet. I'm just sorry they took their anger at me out on—" He covers his face with his other hand.

First time I've ever seen him cry.

"I told you—it didn't work," I say, but between the music and his crying, I don't think he hears me. I wrap my arms around him instead. His shoulders tremble.

After a few minutes, he steps back, his hand holding my face. Then he inhales sharply and wipes his eyes. "I can't tell you how good it feels to tell you. The stress has been killing me."

I look at Germ. He has a look in his eye that says, *Don't.* Mom's face is resigned. No sign of shock or surprise. "Did you know about this?"

She nods.

Unbelievable. All these secrets. They're like waves that keep crashing into me, throwing me off balance. I open my mouth to speak but Dad says, "The question is, what now? Where do we go from here?"

"Don't say it, Parker." Mom's tone is stern. "Just don't even—"

"I've seen smuggled photos, Becca. It's not as bad as they say."

"What's not?" I ask.

"Outbound," Dad says dismissively. I remember the conversation with Germ on our way back from Eevee's school. Dad isn't actually considering moving us to the DMZ, is he? "If we stay here," he says, "we'll always be—"

"Look at me!" Mom's voice rises above the music. She motions to her legs. "Look at me. *I can't.*"

"You're right." Dad takes her in his arms and says, "I'm sorry," again and again.

"What if it isn't your fault?" I ask. Germ's eyes go wide and he shakes his head, but I say it anyway. "What if I've been getting their attention?" He throws up his hands and turns away.

Mom and Dad look at me, confused. My head and heart

both pound so hard I feel like I'm about to have a stroke, but I start talking, telling them everything—about Red December and Warren and M chips, and that I'm not their Danny, that I jumped here from another world and that's why I've been acting weird and don't know things, and that I'm sorry for messing it all up but maybe it doesn't matter because I probably won't be able to stay anyway—and I only stop when I run out of words and see Mom's hand tightly gripping Dad's arm. Germ still stands farther off with his back turned. I breathe and wait for that feeling Dad had, that good feeling from getting everything off his chest, but it doesn't come.

"Danny." Dad takes a step toward me. "It's late and you've been through a lot."

Germ turns around, surprised.

"You should get some rest," Mom touches my arm. "We can talk about this again in the morning."

They don't believe me.

They don't believe me.

Later, when they're asleep and I'm not, I turn on the desk light. I can't stop thinking about what I've seen during the episodes. The other Eevee under the stars. That room with the Einstein poster. My old room at the foster house. I wish I knew what was happening there. I wonder if the other Danny senses what's happening here.

The drawer is full of pens, but it takes a few scribbles

to find one that works. I tear a page from a notebook and write.

Danny,

If you're reading this, I'm back in my world again, and you're here in yours. I've been trying to figure out how it works. It has something to do with Skylar, the new surveillance system they're setting up. Every time they test it, you and I meet up between here and there. They're supposed to flip the on switch for good next week. Who knows what will happen then.

I don't blame you for wanting your life back. By now you have a good idea of what I go through there. Maybe you can understand why I don't want to go back, and why I'm fighting so hard to stay. But if you're reading this, then I guess it doesn't matter. You won.

You have it so good, Danny. Mom and Dad. Germ. Eevee. I hope after all of this, when you're with them, you'll remember me. I hope you'll appreciate them and your life.

Don't screw this up, man. And whatever you do, don't hurt Eevee. She's the most amazing thing that's ever happened to either of us. If you hurt her, I swear I'll find some way to reach back through and pound you.

Danny

P.S. Germ knows about the jumping.
P.P.S. Hug Mom. A lot.

I fold the paper in half, write DANNY on the front and leave it tucked under a book. Hopefully, the other Danny will find it and read it and know.

Halfway back to bed, I think of the M chips and Warren's plan. What if I jump back before we're done?

I click the light on again and pull the paper back out. At the bottom, I draw an arrow and write OVER. On the back, under the fold, I scribble out the details of what we're doing, the names of everyone involved and how it's all supposed to work. Germ can catch him up, too. Instead of tucking it under a book, I put it in my sweatshirt pocket. What if I'm not home when I jump? Better safe than sorry.

43

EEVEE

My dress hangs in the closet, waiting for Friday night. My phone sits on the dresser, waiting for him to call. My brush rests in my hand, waiting for direction.

Waiting. Waiting. All this waiting is driving me insane.

I didn't hear from him yesterday. The day came and went, and nothing. Maybe he didn't get my messages. Maybe he was busy with Germ, swapping out M chips. He probably got home late and was too tired to call. I'm sure that's what it was. I'm sure the phone will ring any minute.

My eyes wander from the blank canvas to the place we stood when he touched my face, when he kissed me, when we fell into each other. The memory is like the shock of a flashbulb: always in my eyes. The room feels empty, yet full of him. Of us.

Come on, phone. Ring.

The blankness of this canvas has to go. I close my eyes and imagine his face, inches from mine. Then swap the brush for a pencil and rough-sketch him into canvas fibers. I move my hand along his forehead, down the gentle slope of his cheek. With light strokes, I draw the funny cowlick in his hairline, the bridge of his nose, the length of his eyebrow. Then the eye, the almond shape, his piercing gaze. Adding hints of shadow, I sit back to see how I did. The canvas bears one-quarter of his face. Just the upper right, from forehead to cheekbone, bridge of nose to ear. His eye is the focus. Will I be able to find the right kind of blue?

I trade the pencil for a brush, loading it up with phthalo. I dab in white, coaxing out the color. Over and over, I mix and remix, but the hue is always wrong. Even if I found the right match, I could never capture his spark. No one could. Not even the best painters in the world.

My hands fall into my lap.

I don't want a painting of him.

I want him.

The ringing of the phone startles me. I almost knock the easel over tripping my way to answer it. It must be him. It has to be—

"Eevee."

Vivian's voice is like acid dripped into my ears.

"Now is a good time for you to come work on this painting. The jury is only two days away."

I make the ugliest face I can at her through the phone. Then I say sweetly, "I'll be right over."

44

DANNY

Germ knocks twice on Warren's door, pauses and knocks once more. "You're sure about this?"

I look down the hallway behind us. "Sure as anything."

"That's not saying much."

The door opens a crack and Warren peers out. "Do you feel safe and secure?"

"Um . . ." I look at Germ. "No?"

"Does someone want to harm you?"

"Probably."

"Is compliance good?"

"Oh." I smirk. "I see what you're doing."

"Answer the question."

He's serious. "No. Unless it's compliance to disobedience. But that's kind of an oxymoron."

He narrows his eyes, then disarms the security system and opens the door. As soon as we step into the room, he shuts it again and resets the system.

"How did you know about Hydro?" I ask.

"I have connections. I know things." He looks at his watch. "Listen, we're going to have to keep this short. I have Emergent Programming in fifteen."

"Minutes?" I run a hand through my hair. "Where do I start?"

"The beginning?"

I take a deep breath, but Germ blurts out, "He jumped here in a Swirling Vortex of Doom."

Well, that's one way of getting it done. "Pretty much."

Warren adjusts his glasses. "Maybe roll it back a couple of frames?"

"Okay, this is going to sound crazy," I say, "but this isn't my life. I'm not Danny. I mean, I am, but I'm not. A week and a half ago, I was sitting in class when suddenly this . . . *thing* . . . happened inside me and—"

"He fell through a time tunnel," Germ finishes.

"Well, some kind of a tunnel, and I landed here. Not *here* here. At the mall where those bombs went off. I don't know how it happened, but I think it has something to do with Skylar. That's why we came to talk to you."

"Skylar?" Warren makes a face. "Why would you think that?"

"Does that mean you believe me?"

He shrugs. "I intern at DART. It takes a lot to faze me. You say you're from another Phoenix? Fine, you're from another Phoenix. Whatever trips your trigger. I once heard about a guy who thinks he's Peter Pan. Wears green tights and a funny hat all the time. Now, what's this about Skylar?"

Germ jumps in again. "He thinks that tunnel opens up whenever they test Skylar."

I count off the days on my fingers. "Friday. Wednesday. Monday. Each of those days, I got this buzzing feeling inside and saw glimpses of the Phoenix I'm from. I haven't jumped back, though. Not yet."

"Obviously." Warren slides open the control panel and the room transforms. He crosses to the desk and types on the projected keys. The monitors display the same screens as on Saturday. "When did you say these episodes occurred?"

"Friday, Wednesday and Monday."

"Times?"

"Oh." I think back. "Friday morning around nine. Wednesday happened at the castle, so . . . midnight-ish? And Monday's was around three, I'm guessing."

Warren peers at the monitors. "Well, I'll be a Jammie Dodger."

"It matches up?" I ask, leaning in beside him.

"System-wide tests were run each of those days, and only those days. The times match up as well." He taps a finger on the desk. "How many relay chips have you guys been able to swap out?"

"One," Germ says.

Warren shakes his head. "They've increased security throughout the city for Friday's gala. It's making it difficult to get anything done. Eevee hasn't been able to do *any* of hers yet."

A shiver runs down my arms at the sound of her name. I stopped by her dorm room on the way here, but she didn't answer. She's probably in class, or off painting. Hopefully, she'll find the note.

Warren leans back against the desk. "I think we should tell Mac."

"Who?" Germ and I ask at the same time. Germ mutters, "Jinx."

"Marcus McAllister," Warren says. "Lead architect on Skylar. Maybe we can convince him it poses a physical threat to the population. Could be a useful plan B if the chip virus fails." He grabs a lab coat from the closet. "Let's go."

"What about Emergent Programming?" Germ asks.

"Priorities," he says. "This takes alpha."

The DART lobby is cold, all granite and metal. A woman wearing a headset sits at a wide reception desk. Behind her, the wall flows with a circulating waterfall. Her only acknowledgment of us is one raised eyebrow. Warren saunters up to the desk, but we hang back, pretending to be interested in the huge driftwood sculpture on the wall.

"This place gives me the creeps," Germ mutters. "What if it's a trap?"

"I've already been through Hydro. What's the worst they could do?"

"Do you really want to know?"

"No." I look past him. "Here he comes."

Warren holds out two clip-on badges. "You guys need to keep these on and visible at all times. Mac will be out in a minute." He lowers his voice. "Probably best to keep the parallel-dimension talk in the deep freeze."

"Parallel what?" I ask.

"Dimensions. You know, your Phoenix, our Phoenix?" He says it like he's talking about what he ate for lunch.

Germ and I follow him to a conference room off the lobby. Inside is a long mahogany table. We take the three chairs at the nearest end. They're squishy. Germ swivels back and forth in his until Warren gives him a look. A door at the far end of the room opens and a tall guy walks in. He wears a lab coat over his jeans and plaid work shirt, the sleeves pushed up to his elbows. When he extends his hand, he says, "Dr. Marcus McAllister. You can call me Mac." He sits at the head of the table and rests his arms across his stomach. "What brings you gentlemen out today? Warren, don't you have morning classes?"

"Yes," Warren says, "but something more pressing has come up. These are friends of mine from Kierland Academy. Danny has possible evidence Skylar could pose a public health risk."

Mac gives a dismissive laugh. "That's highly unlikely."

"Which was my thought, too," Warren continues, "until he explained his symptoms and when they occurred."

Mac turns toward me, his face curious. "Okay. Let's hear these *symptoms.*"

"Um." I think through how much to say, hoping Germ doesn't interrupt. "Well, there's a tightness in my chest, and it feels like my lungs are freezing from the inside." I sound like such a crazy person that I'm surprised this guy hasn't walked out. "Then I get a buzzing feeling, like ants are crawling all over me. Oh, and I hear static in my ears."

"Static."

"Yes, sir."

"Have you sought the opinion of a medical professional?"

"Uh . . . no, sir."

Mac tents his fingers under his chin. "And why do you suspect these symptoms are related to Skylar?"

Warren jumps in, and I'm grateful for the breather. "Well, that's the fascinating part. His symptoms occurred in conjunction with every Skylar system test."

"What about Skylar would cause such symptoms? It doesn't make sense."

"I'm wondering the same thing," Warren says. "Maybe it's some kind of hypersensitivity to the EMF waves? Regardless, I think it's prudent to conduct a test. He could be one of many experiencing symptoms. Better to recognize it now than after rollout, if I may say so, and face public backlash."

Mac drums his fingers on the arm of his chair, his eyes shifting between Warren and me. Then he pulls out his phone. "Lydia, I'm going to need expedited security clearance for two individuals."

●

We follow Mac through a brightly lit room filled with computer workstations and racks of equipment and with bundled wires tracked across the ceiling to a smaller room full of DART employees sitting at terminals. The walls are covered in huge screens, displaying the same things we saw in Warren's dorm room. Mac leans over one of the desks and activates the keyboard with his security badge. "The shortest distance between two points is a straight line." He steps back to let Warren take the controls. Meanwhile, a lab tech leads me to a chair and attaches electrode pads to my chest and back. I watch my heart make blips across the monitor screen. Is it fast? It seems fast, but then, I am nervous. I take a deep breath and the blips slow down. Better.

Mac raises his voice and all the employees give him their attention. "Listen up, folks. We're going to run a phase one diagnostic. Please ready your stations." The energy of the room changes as employees take position. He lays a hand on Warren's shoulder. "Set it for five."

Warren's fingers race over the keyboard. "Ready."

Mac walks to where I'm sitting and crosses his arms. He looks confident. Proud. "Sit back and enjoy the show."

A clock appears in the corner of the largest screen, counting down in milliseconds.

Five.

Four.

Germ looks as freaked out as I feel.

Three.

I grip the arms of the chair.

Two.

One.

The screens switch to a skeletal view of the city and cold races across my chest. Yellow circles and red Xs swim in my eyes. My jaw clenches, my muscles go taut, and through the static I hear Germ yelling.

But instead of the tunnel and the pull, everything fades.

When I open my eyes, I'm on my knees surrounded by DART employees staring down at me. One switches off the alarm on the heart monitor.

I never saw the other Phoenix. Never felt the other Danny.

"Shut it all the way down." Mac's face iş pale. The confidence is gone. He stands with one hand on his hip and runs the other over his face. In a loud voice, he says, "Someone get me Governor Solomon on the phone."

45

EEVEE

I push my door open with my elbow and, once inside, bump it closed again with my hip. Everything's a mess, just like it's been since I got back from shopping with Mom on Tuesday. Here it is Thursday and I don't even know where the time went. Oh, wait. Yes, I do. It went to Vivian. The art supplies tumble from my arms onto the bed, and I flop down beside them, exhausted. I don't even glance at my phone. I already know he hasn't called.

"So," I say to the girl in the painting on the easel, "how was your day?"

She doesn't say anything back, of course.

Her face is shiny, the oils still wet. I painted her in a hurry this morning, in the little time I had between breakfast and going back to Vivian's. She's full of angst and frustration, her eyes fierce like her blazing-fire hair. The Art Guild would never approve, but that's okay. She's not for them. She's for me.

I pick up my palette and brush, thin out burnt umber and

pull it through her hair. My arms are tired, but painting her, I find my own fire again.

Tomorrow is the jury deadline and Vivian's paintings look great. Maybe she's even learned something, watching me do all the work for her. Somehow I doubt it, though. Just like I doubt she's thought about what will happen when she gets to Belford and they discover she's a fraud. But that's not my problem, right?

I smirk and grow the flames higher. Then my eyes move to the remains of *Confidante* tucked away in the bag on the coffee table. No, my problems are something else entirely.

"What do you think?" I ask the flame-haired girl. "Should I do it?"

Her eyes are severe, like a dare.

I slide open my closet door and search through bins of art supplies until I find a spool of thin gold wire. In a separate bin, beneath a bag of Popsicle sticks, I find the cutters and the pin tool from my sculpting set.

Time to reclaim what I've lost.

46

DANNY

I listen to the phone ringing and tell myself not to worry. There's a logical reason she's not picking up. She hasn't been thrown into the back of a van. She's the governor's daughter. They wouldn't put her in—

"Hello?"

I jolt upright. "Eevee?"

"Danny! Oh my God, it's you."

"Are you okay?"

"Yeah." She sounds both panicked and relieved. "Sorry. I was working and didn't hear the phone ringing. Are you okay? I've left you so many messages."

"I know. I'm sorry. It's just . . . things have been kinda crazy."

"Same here." She pauses. "Actually, I was starting to wonder if you were dodging me."

"What? No. Didn't you get my note?"

"Note?" Her breathing changes as she moves through her room.

"I stopped by yesterday, but you weren't there, so I left a note under your door."

"You were *here?*" She makes a frustrated growl. "Figures I'd be out. Hang on." I hear her moving things. "Such a mess. No wonder I didn't see— Oh!" There's the sound of paper, and she says, "You came to see me," like she can't believe it.

"I did."

"You weren't dodging me."

"Of course not." I fall back on the bed and exhale. "So, what are you working on?"

"A new art project. Well, kind of new. It's a little hard to explain."

"Try me."

"You know the bits of painting I scavenged from the fire? I'm trying to stitch them back together using wire."

"That sounds cool."

"I guess so." She yawns. "It feels good to try something different. What about you?"

"I haven't been painting at all."

"You know what I mean." I can hear her smiling. Wish I could see it, too. "What have you been up to?"

I let silence settle between us as I sift through everything that's happened since I last saw her. I want to tell her about Hydro and Dad's confession, about the Skylar test—and most of all, about me—but Warren warned us about sharing information over the phone.

"Danny? Are you still there?"

"Yeah. Sorry."

"Have you and Germ been able to—"

"Only one. It's been . . . difficult." Better change the subject. "But enough about that. What about you? You've been super busy."

"Yeah." She still sounds concerned. "I've been, um, doing a lot of painting."

"That's great."

"Not really," she says. "It's all crazy stuff. My weird ideas. Not anything I can actually show. The jury is tomorrow, and . . ." She sighs. "I'm not going to do it."

"What? Why not?"

"I can't submit this stuff. It's different."

"Different is good. What would the world be like if everything was the same?"

"Not everyone thinks that." She doesn't say anything for a long time, then, "I miss you."

Her voice shivers through me. "I miss you, too."

"Wish I could see you." She sounds sleepy.

"I could come over."

"Curfew."

"Screw curfew."

"We'll see each other tomorrow."

"Well, I wish tomorrow would hurry up and get here."

"Me too."

The line goes quiet and I wonder if she's fallen asleep. Then she says, "Is all of this worth it?"

The question hangs there between us. "It will be," I say at last. "It has to be."

47

EEVEE

My phone alarm startles me awake, stuck under my face and blaring in my ear. I peel it away and squint at the screen. *Art Guild jury,* it reads, *begins in one hour.*

Great. I'd set it weeks ago, thinking I'd need to be up bright and early this morning, and forgot to cancel it.

I untangle my feet from the covers and sit up, taking in the damage from the night before. Bits of wire and canvas lie strewn around the floor. Tubes of paint lie uncapped and drying. The cup of brushes lies on its side, knocked over in my dive for the phone. Brushes surround it like a motionless explosion.

When did we hang up? I don't remember saying goodbye. Wait. It's Friday. I get to see him tonight.

The flame-haired girl watches as I walk to the sink and splash water on my face. I'm a wreck. It's going to take a lot of work to pull me together for the gala.

I grab a soda from the mini-fridge and tiptoe through the

mess to sit in the chair, my legs tucked up under me. Morning light peeks in around the edges of the blinds and glints off the gold paint on the resurrected *Confidante*. The wire stitching looks macabre, especially with the sooty raw canvas edges. It's weird. Different.

Different is good.

His words last night caught me off guard. For a moment I actually thought about submitting these paintings to the jury. How crazy would that be?

I down the rest of the soda and go to the closet to pack for the big weekend downtown.

The flame-haired girl watches me pull out my overnight bag.

"No," I tell her as I pack.

"Shut up," as I get dressed.

"Stop looking at me," as I brush my teeth.

"It's a bad idea," as I gather my toiletries.

I pull the red dress from the closet and turn to find myself eye to eye with the other girl, the one emerging from the dark. Her hands reach for me. "Don't you start." My gaze follows the flame-haired girl's to the coffee table, where my newest creation lies.

These paintings are my breath. My soul. They represent not only what I can do but who I am.

Different.

What would the world be like if everything was the same?

I swallow, feeling the fire of Danny's words. A little voice in my head says, *You'll be sorry.*

Damn these Moments, making me choose.

"Fine." A quick check of the time shows I'll have only

minutes to spare if I hurry. I load the flame-haired girl, the girl emerging from the dark, the fractured Danny watercolor, an older one of people evaporating into butterflies, and the wire-stitched *Confidante* into my portfolio case, then leave before fear or reason can stop me.

48

DANNY

Dad woke me early with a tap on my bedroom door. "Let's go."
I rolled over and realized I was still holding the phone in my
hand.

They've opened the harbor for gala-weekend festivities.
Dad wasted no time getting the boat ready. We moved through
the same procedure as before, packing drinks and snacks and
kissing Mom before heading out.

The roads were a mess. Checkpoints at every turn. Even
when the traffic picked up, Dad kept it five under. Anything
to avoid unwanted attention.

But we made it.

Waves splash against the boat as we move slowly toward
the open sea. The rocking motion makes my head feel strange.
The harbor grows small behind us, and ahead is rolling blue.
Oil rigs dot the horizon, gray with haze. Now and then security
buzzes us in their speedboats, and Dad mutters, "Go away."

This is the ocean.

I'm in a boat. With my dad. On the ocean.

He lifts the cooler lid and pulls out two cans of soda. Pops one open and hands the other to me. "Your granddad used to bring me out here when I was your age." He takes a drink and sits down. "He'd call in sick for me and we'd come out here. Fish. Talk. 'Never spend a day inside,' he'd say, 'if you can spend it out at sea.'" He leans his elbows back on the engine house and looks out over the water. He's quiet a long time, like he's thinking. Remembering, maybe. I sit back and watch a Jet Ski in the distance bouncing across the waves.

"Remember the time we went camping up by Woods Canyon?" he asks. "Took the rowboat out on the lake?"

"Of course." I take a sip of soda. The Jet Ski slows, turns, races back the way it came.

"When those storm clouds came up so quickly, and the lightning started striking the trees around us?" He shakes his head. "I thought, What have you done, Ogden, taking your son out in a metal boat during a thunderstorm? And your eyes." He laughs. "Whenever lightning flashed, your eyes were like saucers." He does an impression of me and laughs again, slapping his leg. "Good times. Remember?"

I smile. "Yeah. Good times."

He drums a rhythm with his ring finger against the soda can. "Didn't happen."

"What?" My eyes snap to his face.

"It didn't happen." He leans forward, his elbows on his knees. "No rowboat. No thunderstorm."

Oh.

He drains what's left of his drink. "Your, uh, story. What

you said after you got back the other night, about being from somewhere else. That was true, wasn't it."

"Yes."

His head drops to his hands, and he rubs his face as he lifts it again. "Tell me about it."

"About jumping here?"

He shakes his head. "About the other world. About you."

I look away. This is the part I've been dreading. "Um, well . . . It's different there," I say. "No ocean, for starters."

"Really?" He looks baffled. "Wow."

"It's a desert, actually. Cactus. Coyotes. Really hot summers." I can tell he's trying to imagine what I'm telling him. "Sunshine. Lots of sunshine."

"But you. What about you?"

"I don't know. I'm just Danny."

He prompts me for more, so I close my eyes and dredge up the images I've worked so hard to forget.

And I tell him.

A couple of times he looks like he'd rather jump out of the boat than hear what I'm saying, but he listens until I'm done and it's all there, out in the open. We sit in silence, just the sound of the waves.

"He's trying to come back," I say. "The other Danny. *Your* Danny. When the vortex opens, I can feel him trying to push across." I swallow the knot in my throat. "When it happens again, I won't fight. He should be here, where he belongs."

"*My* Danny?" He gives his head a small shake and puts a hand on my knee. "You're my Danny. You both are. If you leave, I'll know you're there, without Mom and me. Just like

I know he's there now, on his own." He exhales. "Please don't tell your mother. Not any of it. She's convinced it was the Hydro talking the other night. If she hears this, I don't know what it'll do to her."

"I won't say anything." I watch a seagull gliding in the breeze. "Dad? What do we do now?"

He thinks a moment, then says, "We keep going. Appreciate the time we have. Live each day the best we can."

"Do you think that's what Danny would want?"

"I think that's what anyone would want," he says. "In any world."

49

EEVEE

A million thoughts banter about in my mind as I walk through the doors of the Juniper Gallery in the North Building on campus. The loudest of them: Am I really going to do this?

This is what I dreamed about for so long. What I worked for years to achieve. This is the moment the Art Guild was going to see I'm a serious and talented artist and, most of all, a sure investment.

All of that would be true of this moment *if.* If my paintings hadn't been ruined. If there hadn't been a fire. If I hadn't met Danny Ogden.

Seems too small a word to carry such heavy repercussions.

The regular exhibits are gone, replaced by modular walls waiting to be adorned. Students bustle around, lugging paintings, hanging and straightening them, affixing labels. At the far wall, I see Vivian and Antonio. She looks nervous, biting her thumbnail as she works on her display. I choose a wall at the opposite corner, as far from her as I can get.

Taking a deep breath, I set my stuff down and pull the paintings out of the portfolio case. As I look at each one, I'm filled with a sense of pride. And dread.

"You," I say, picking up the flame-haired girl, "will be front and center." Her shocking orange head will grab attention, that's for sure. I arrange the other paintings around her, switching their placements for best effect, testing them for eye flow. I choose the upper left corner for *Confidante,* and hang the butterflies at the far right so they look like they're flying off the wall. I realize too late I don't have information labels for the pieces. Oh well. It's not like the members of the Art Guild are going to be writing any of them down anyway.

"Do you have a submission form?" a woman asks. Her Art Guild name tag says SUSAN. She sees my work and takes a sucking breath through her teeth.

"No, I don't." I smile. "Thank you." She hands me the form and walks away.

I fill in my name, contact information and schooling and mentorship information and check the box verifying the work is original and mine. There are two blanks for signatures, one for me and one for Antonio. I sign my name and walk to the far side of the room.

"Such progress," I hear Antonio saying. Vivian sees me approaching and her eyes narrow.

I clear my throat. "Excuse me, Antonio?"

His face brightens when he sees me. "*Compagna!* You are here! I gave up hope on you."

"Sorry." I hold out the form. "I, um, need you to sign my submission form."

"Oh yes, yes." He takes the form and points to Vivian. "Yours too."

She completes hers quickly, not even hesitating as she checks the box saying she isn't committing fraud. I'm tempted to say how nice my work looks in her display, but I don't. What would be the point?

"Where are you set up?" Antonio asks.

"Over there." My vision telescopes as I lead him to the far wall. It's the longest walk of my life. Antonio takes his time moving through the exhibits, talking to students and other teachers. At one point he announces loudly that everyone should join him in seeing the display of his top student. The voice in my head screams, *You'll be sorry. You'll be sorry.*

I stop in front of my display, fold my arms and wait. Antonio arrives with a small crowd of onlookers eager to see what the fuss is about. I watch his face as he takes in each piece. He leans in close to *Confidante*—realizing what it used to be, I'm sure—and lingers last on the flame-haired girl. His eyebrows twitch and his hand crushes my submission form. Then he turns and walks away, tossing the paper in the air. It falls to the floor at my feet.

You'll be sorry.

Maybe, but what's done is done. I pick up the form and brush it off before pinning it to the wall. Then I grab my belongings and leave everyone standing there, gaping.

50

DANNY

I walk past the limos lined up in front of the Regency Majestic and wonder who's behind all those tinted windows. They're probably looking out, wondering who walks to a gala in a suit borrowed from his dad's closet.

The last time I wore a suit was never. I sure hope Eevee appreciates this.

Eevee. Her name alone makes my feet move faster.

The porter opens a limo door and offers his hand to a woman in a shimmery dress. She waits for her date, and the two walk the red carpet into the hotel. I follow, ducking away when cameras begin to flash.

The lobby is unlike anything I've ever seen. Mosaic floors lead to an enormous rotunda encircled by marble pillars. Two spiral staircases curve along the walls, rising to an upper level, where the ceiling is lit by hundreds of starburst chandeliers. I keep to the carpet, descending a small flight of stairs toward a crowded bar and restaurant. Ahead is a series of metal detectors, scanners and pat-downs. The usual. There's a bit of a holdup when a woman won't allow her purse to be searched, but she finally hands it over and we're all on our way again.

I walk through a set of double doors into an enormous ballroom. Chandeliers as big as cars hang from the ceiling. White-and-gold flower arrangements decorate the walls, tables and stage, their scent mixing with the smells of alcohol and expensive perfume. A band in the corner plays jazzy music while men in tuxedos mingle with women in gowns. I'm a sardine in a sea of penguins.

A waiter walks by with a tray of champagne glasses. I snag one and gulp half of it down. Somewhere in this mass of humanity is my date. My eyes scan the crowd. If I were the governor's daughter, where would I be?

With the governor, of course.

I see her across the room, standing between her mom and dad, wearing a red dress. Her hair is up and her shoulders are bare. She smiles and gestures as she talks to a couple.

She's stunning.

I down the rest of the glass and add it to the tray of a passing waiter. The great thing about being a nobody in this kind of crowd is that it takes me no time at all to cross the room. I slip around groups of chattering women and couples dancing, then join her circle. I lean my head toward her and say, "Hi."

When she realizes it's me, she gasps and grabs me in a hug. Her mom smiles. Her dad does not.

"Good evening, Governor Solomon," I say, extending my hand. He looks me up and down before shaking it.

"Mom, Dad, this is Danny." Eevee slips her arm around mine. "Danny, this is my mom and dad."

"Nice to meet you," Mom says.

"You too," I say.

I turn to Eevee to tell her how amazing she looks, but she speaks first. "And this is Senator Hayes and his wife, Elana."

"Oh," I say, shaking their hands. "Nice to meet you."

They smile and I smile and it all gets a little awkward until Eevee says, "Ooh, are those hors d'oeuvres?" She steers me away. When we're out of earshot, she laughs. "Your face!" She makes a stunned face and laughs again as we maneuver toward a tall table loaded with tiny bites of food. Bacon-wrapped beef medallions. Salmon canapés. Handmade ravioli. Caviar. It's endless, and the waiters keep bringing out more.

"Do you have any idea how far outside my comfort zone I am here?" I say, chowing down on a stuffed mushroom.

"Do you have any idea how good you look?"

"Me? You look . . ." I give up words for hand signals. Mind-blowing.

"Thank you." She runs her hands down her dress. "Does it remind you of anything?"

"Uh . . . I don't know. Does it?" I'm thinking about her hips.

"The museum." She gives her head a little shake, then looks around the room. "Do you have any idea how bad I want to get my hands on you?"

"So what's stopping you?"

"Only about three hundred and fifty people. Smile." She rests her hand on my arm and we both smile as a photographer snaps our picture. I'm pretty sure I have food in my teeth.

"Let's go somewhere, then." I start looking for exits.

"I *can't*. I'm on the clock." Her expression changes and she grabs my arm. "Oh no."

"What?" I turn and see a blond girl approaching.

"Hi, Eevee," she says, with one of those catty smiles that girls give when they really hate each other. "Who's your date?"

Eevee glares at her a moment, then puts on the fakery, too. "Vivian, this is Danny. Danny, Vivian Hayes, Senator Hayes's daughter."

"Oh," I say, shaking her hand, "I just met your parents."

She smiles at me like, *Isn't that nice?* and turns to Eevee. "Curious display this morning. I'm sure the Art Guild found your paintings interesting, to say the least."

"I'm sure they loved yours."

"Well, Antonio did say he overheard some members saying my work was outstanding."

"If anyone's art is *outstanding,*" I say, making the word sound as snooty as I can, "it's this girl's right here." I lean over and kiss Eevee on the cheek. She looks embarrassed. Maybe I shouldn't have done that.

Vivian raises an eyebrow. "I guess we'll see, won't we?" And she walks away.

"What was that about?" I ask. "Didn't you say you weren't doing the jury exhibit?"

"I wasn't," she says, finally taking her eyes off Vivian. "But at the last minute, I had this crazy idea."

"You entered the paintings that were in your room, didn't you?"

She nods. "I thought it would be cool to take a stand. Show them who I really am. But now . . ." She shrugs.

"Are you kidding? I think that's incredible. And so brave."

"Or stupid."

As she's telling me about the morning, my head gets this weird feeling, like the floor is moving, like I'm still out on the ocean with Dad. I hold on to the table, expecting the cold and the static to start up. Maybe it's just the champagne I drank. Hopefully, that's all it is.

I put my hands on her arms and look her in the eye. "I'm so sorry. Stay here. I promise I'll be right back." And I walk out of the ballroom, tugging at my collar. On the far side of the entrance is a large square pillar. I lean back against it and breathe, praying I'm not about to jump.

Voices speak low on the other side of the pillar and the word *December* catches my ear. "He knows it wasn't us, so now he thinks there's a real cell at work."

"And you're playing it up?"

"Of course. The more paranoid he is, the more mistakes he'll make."

"Things could still work in his favor if the rollout is successful."

"That won't matter. If people don't show, great. If they do, we run a false flag that exploits the system's weaknesses. Either way, we win."

Even though my head is still wonky, I slink away from the pillar. Whatever they were talking about, it didn't feel right to listen. From the corner of my eye, I watch the two men. One leaves. The other turns to walk back into the ballroom. It's Senator Hayes.

I find a restroom and splash water on my face, trying to get my head together before going back in. "Not now," I mutter at my reflection, expecting the floor to open and swallow me down.

It takes me a minute to find her again in the ballroom. She's been trapped by a couple of women and a towering flower arrangement. She excuses herself and makes a beeline for me. "You're back, finally! Everything okay?" She adjusts my tie and rests her hand on my chest.

"Yeah. I just got overwhelmed. Needed to breathe."

She rolls her eyes. "Welcome to my world."

The band stops playing and someone up on the stage taps the microphone. The speeches are about to start.

She slips her hand into mine. "Let's get out of here."

51

EEVEE

I lead him through the crowd around the stage. This is always the dullest part of the gala. They'll blab on for an hour at least. No one will notice we're gone.

We exit the ballroom and take a left, passing the bar and heading for the patio. He holds the door open for me, brushing my shoulder as I walk through. The night air raises goose bumps on my arms. It's less crowded out here than in the ballroom, but there are still so many people lounging around the fire pits. Too bad. A fire would be nice.

We walk hand in hand down the steps toward the pool. On the far side, the seating is more secluded. Darker too. As soon as we pass the corner of a shrouded cabana, his arm moves around my waist and his lips touch the back of my neck. Dizzy, I turn and slip my hands inside his coat. My fingers run down his back and sides as his hands search out my hips, my neck, the small of my back. He pulls me close, lifting me to kiss my neck, my collarbone. I melt into him, and in a heartbeat, the days of separation dissolve away, taking with them all the stress and care and worry. We're together, and we're free.

But then he stops, resting his forehead against mine, our lips barely touching. His breath is warm against my skin. His eyes are closed.

"What's wrong?"

"I think I'm running out of time."

"We have all night." I kiss him again, but he holds back and takes my hand.

"Eevee, there's something I need to tell you."

My stomach cartwheels. "Wait. You're breaking up with me?"

"No." He traces his finger along my jawline. "You were so brave today, sharing your secret art with the world. I just . . . I'm tired of keeping my secret from you." He swallows hard. "Eevee, I'm not who you think I am."

I take a small step back. "What?"

His eyes never leave mine as he tells me about another world, another him—another *me,* even. It's fantastical and bizarre and awful and there's no way any of it could be true because it's ridiculous and that's not how the world works. I blink, my mind racing. "No, that's impossible. We met outside the museum the night of Bosca's exhibit."

"That wasn't me."

"Yes, it was," I say, trying to keep my voice down. "I should know. I kissed you."

"You kissed him."

"Who?"

"The other Danny."

"Oh my God." I pull away from him. "Why are you doing this?"

"Because . . ." He rubs the heels of his hands into his eyes. "I think it's going to happen again, and I want you to know in case it does."

He takes a step toward me, but I hold up my hands. "I don't know why you're doing this, but I think you should just—"

I don't give him the chance to leave. I leave him instead, stumbling back through the crowds of people swarming the lobby, to the cars waiting in the hotel drive. Jonas takes one look at my face and opens the rear passenger door. I climb in, curl into the backseat and fall apart. The engine starts and we drive away. He doesn't say anything, but even if he did, it would all be wrong. The voice in my head returns. *You'll be sorry.*

52

DANNY

She left.

I grab a glass from a waiter on the patio. And another from a tray in the lobby. Pound a few more until the floor is no longer flat. I stumble into the ballroom, hell-bent on kicking up trouble.

But something stops me.

No.

Some*one*.

He grabs my arms and steers me out to the lobby. My head flops back and I stare up at the stars falling from the ceiling above. Angry shouting pounds in my ears. Frightened faces blur in my eyes. Bits of white paper float down from the upper level and scatter across the mosaic floor. What do they say? My head falls forward, but he holds me tight. I fight against him and reach down to snag one. The bar-code-head guy screaming. Everywhere I look, the bar-code-head guy screaming. I crumple the flyer in my fist as he walks me off the carpet, his hands holding me up, his brown shoes pounding the marble. My own feet stumble, confused. Outside, he practically carries me to the car. Opens the door, pushes me inside, drives me away.

53

EEVEE

Saturday morning, I wake up in my bed at the Executive Tower with my feet tangled in the sheets and a headache throbbing behind my eyes. I wish for stars, but above me there's just a blank white ceiling. One look at my dress lying in a heap on the floor and the sadness comes flooding back. The clock reads 10:23. I force myself up, change into yoga pants and a T-shirt and shuffle off in search of water.

The place is empty. No sign of life. My steps through the hall are the only sound. Must have been quite a party last night. Everyone is still sleeping it off.

My mind slips into the memory of his lips and hands, his eyes looking into mine. I try to shake it away, but my heart is a sinkhole caving in. I grip the back of a chair and my shoulders shake as tears stream silently down my face. It was supposed to be a perfect night. But instead, it's all in pieces. Just like everything else in my—

Someone else is awake. I walk toward the kitchen, wiping

my eyes, and hear Dad say, "I'm telling you, they're out there. Something has to be done."

Richard responds, but his voice is too low to make out what he says. I inch closer to the door.

"How am I supposed to secure a city when I can't keep jackasses from crashing my own event?"

Something must have happened after I left last night. Something bad.

"I want it switched on," Dad says. "Now."

Richard says something about public safety.

Dad gets angry. "I don't care what he says. Skylar is a go. If McAllister doesn't agree, he can find another job."

Richard mumbles again. I press my ear to the door. Dad says, "Find out who's behind these events. I don't want to get caught with my pants around my ankles if there's an actual threat."

There's movement behind the door. Quickly, I duck back out into the hallway, then retrace my steps toward the kitchen. The door where I'd just been listening opens, and both Richard and Dad walk out. They look surprised to see me.

"Good morning, honey," Dad says. "Did you sleep well?"

54

Danny

Pain pulls me from my sleep. My head feels like it's coming apart, my eyes like they're glued shut. I force one open and squint. Everything hurts. I peer into the light until the room comes into focus.

How did I get home? Through the haze I remember brown shoes on red carpet, car doors slamming. What happened?

Then it all comes back.

I told her. And she left.

My head falls back into the mattress and one arm flops down to the floor.

I blew it. I had it all. Everything was right there in my hands, and I blew it.

Fighting through the pain, I push myself up. One thing's for sure: This Danny is a lightweight. My head feels drier than desert dirt. I fumble along the hallway to the kitchen and pour myself a glass of water. On the table is the morning paper. The headline declares GALA DISASTER. Photos show panicked people frozen midstep as they leave the hotel. The floor around them is littered with pieces of paper. An inset shows a close-up of the flyer, and a smaller headline reads GRAFFITI FLYER MYSTERY.

What happened? I turn the pages, scanning the photos for a glimpse of Eevee, but she's not there. I hope that means she left before all of this happened.

She left. I flop into a chair and hold the glass to my forehead. If only she'd listened. If only I'd said it all better.

"Look what the cat dragged in," Dad says, walking into the kitchen.

I slide the paper across the table. "Did you see this?"

"Didn't need to," he says, pouring a cup of coffee. "You don't remember me bringing you home?"

I look up at him, surprised. "That was you?"

He raises an eyebrow. "Next time, lay off the booze."

"No kidding."

"So," he says, sitting across from me. He swirls a spoon in his mug. Every *ting* is like a nail in my brain. "Things didn't go well with your date?"

"You could say that." I turn another page. More photos, more stories and still no sign of her. *Gala disrupted in serious security breach,* one article reads. *Masked protesters infiltrated the Regency Majestic . . . disseminated subversive propaganda . . . hotel searched for explosives . . . minor injuries reported . . . governor and his family safe . . .*

Safe. My eyes lock in on the word, but it doesn't quiet the fear rattling around inside. I want to see her, hold her, know for sure she's okay. I close my eyes and relive the moment she pulled away, the look on her face as she disappeared into the crowd. Everything after blurs in a fog of alcohol and confusion. "Wait—why were *you* there?"

He sips his coffee and sets the mug back down. "I was looking out for you."

"Because of this?" I point at the paper.

"I tried to talk you out of going," he says, his voice low, "but I knew the more I pushed, the more you'd run right to it. You're like me that way."

"But I don't get it. How did you know?"

He slides the paper toward himself, scans the stories, then slides it back with his finger pointing at two words: *antigovernment protesters*.

"Is that the group—"

He puts a finger to his lips and tips his head toward the back door. I follow him outside, crossing the cold patio into the colder grass. The air clears my head a little, but my eyes water from the change in light. He stops in the middle of the yard and looks around before saying, "They were planning something big. I already wasn't okay with the idea, but when you announced you were going to the gala, I knew I had to do something."

"That's why they kicked you out, isn't it?" I say, remembering his confession after the Hydro. "Because you tried to stop the plan for the gala."

He nods. "I went down there last night just in case they stuck to their original plan. When security started searching for bombs, I grabbed you and got the hell out." He sighs and looks back toward the house. "What a messed-up world, huh?"

"I don't know," I say, shrugging. "My guess is every world has its problems."

He looks at me for a moment, then shakes his head.

"Dad," I say, stopping him as he starts to walk back to the house. "Thanks for looking out for me."

"Of course," he says. "You're my son."

55

EEVEE

I hide away in my room with my Retrogressives book, ignoring his messages on my phone. But my sadness and confusion run so deep that not even van Gogh can save me. Whenever my mind wanders to him, wondering where he is or what he's doing, I remember his lies. So many lies. I let myself dwell on all of the times he fooled me into believing what wasn't true. Being the governor's daughter complicates things. It's difficult to know who to trust. When it's finally time to leave for school on Monday morning, I throw my stuff into my overnight bag. I leave the red dress hanging in the closet.

The Executive Tower buzzes with activity. It seems every government official is either here in person or on the phone. Dad's advisors pace the halls. They hardly notice me passing.

I stop at the door to Dad's office. He's leaning back on his desk, arms folded, surrounded by officials. Everyone is talking at once. Senator Hayes taps him on the arm and points at me.

"Excuse me, gentlemen," Dad says, "but this young lady needs my attention." He walks over, a sad smile on his face. "Heading back to school?"

I nod and glance at all the people. "What's going on?"

"Nothing you need to be concerned about." He steers me into the hallway. "Listen, I'm sorry your night didn't turn out the way you wanted."

"I'm sorry yours didn't either."

He looks over his shoulder and lowers his voice. "Honey, I think it's best if you stick around school for a while, at least until things settle down." Then he hugs me and says, "Don't worry, though. I've alerted security to keep an eye on you."

When Jonas and I are a few blocks from the Tower, I see why.

DPC forces move in teams, rounding up people from businesses and homes. Men, women, children. They wait in long lines, single file, for their turn at the mobile registration units. All those Unknowns soon to be Knowns. I roll down my window. Sirens echo, ricocheting off the skyscrapers. A female voice repeats directions over the PA system. "Proceed in an orderly fashion to the nearest DPC checkpoint. Your compliance is required."

Neither Jonas nor I say anything as we drive through the streets. He only looks at me once in the rearview. When he does, his eyes are worried.

Farther out, protesters gather in approved areas cordoned off and guarded by soldiers. A parking lot here. A dirt lot there. Angry and shouting, they pound against the chain-link fencing and raise signs into the air. I'm surprised they aren't all carted away. I'm surprised they think their protesting will make any difference. But then, I was naive enough to think I could change the world, too.

56

DANNY

Monday afternoon, Mom walks into the kitchen, holding a piece of paper. "This was on the front door."

"What is it?" Dad asks, and she hands it to him. I get up from the couch and join them at the table.

When the announcement came blaring over the radio and TV this morning, I freaked. Out of nowhere, a female voice had said the city was on lockdown. It's crazy that they can just do that—decide no one is allowed to leave the house, go to work, go to the mailbox, play in the backyard. So here we sit, listening to trucks rumble up and down the street, trying to pretend we aren't all going crazy from the pressure and the not knowing.

"We have until sundown tomorrow to register with Skylar," Dad says, letting the paper fall from his hands. He rubs his forehead. Mom throws her own hands up in frustration.

So that's that. Mac's attempt to shut down Skylar over safety concerns failed. Our plan to take out the system with

M chips failed. Anytime now, Skylar will be switched on, I'll jump back to the other world, and this one will be clamped down in a state of constant surveillance.

Government wins. We lose.

Another truck rumbles by. Mom stops pacing and goes to the window. Dad picks up a pen and doodles on the Sunday paper still lying where I left it yesterday. Gripping the pen, he gives Governor Solomon a black eye and draws a pointed tail on the back of Senator Hayes. The conversation I overheard outside the ballroom drifts into my mind.

If people don't show, great. If they do, we run a false flag that exploits the system's weaknesses. Either way, we win.

"What does 'false flag' mean?"

Dad doesn't look up. He's now defaced almost every picture on the front page. "Uh . . ." He moves to the inset photo of the flyer, transforming the bar-code-head guy into a skull. "It's when a group sets up an attack on its own people but blames someone else. Why?"

Thoughts begin to shift like puzzle pieces in my brain. At the castle, Germ accused Neil of trying to have us killed. Neil said it wasn't Red December. He said he didn't know who it was. *He knows it wasn't us,* the guy talking to Hayes said. *He thinks there's a real cell at work.*

Dad tosses the pen down and walks into the living room. I scoot the paper over and look at Hayes through the doodles. *Either way, we win.*

I turn the pages, searching for the face of the other man. It's difficult to see now that they've been scribbled over with blue ink. Finally, I find him in a small photo on page 3. In the caption is his name: Richard Tremblay, Governor Solomon's chief of staff.

The last puzzle piece clicks into place.

They set up the attack on Patriot Day so people would agree to sign up for Skylar.

"Dad," I say, pushing myself up from the table. "I think I figured something—" But the words catch in my throat as my chest burns with ice. All I hear is static. My eyes cloud over and a girl's voice says, "I don't know." I see a dark outline of her hair, but it's like looking through fogged-up glass. I feel Danny there, too, but it's different this time. Instead of him pushing me out of the way, we're both trying to stand in the same space. My skin feels tight. Cold shivers through me. Then the fog clears and my eyes begin to focus.

I'm in a room. Another kitchen. The walls pulse and everything glows with a halo. Books lie open on the table. She's leaning toward me, her hand on my knee, her face inches from mine.

"Danny?! Danny, no!"

Her voice hits me like a sledgehammer. It's the other Eevee. She doesn't want him to go.

I push against him, knock him back so hard it knocks me back, too. As I fall, I feel the tightness leave me. I land hard on the floor, my chest rippling with cold. Mom and Dad kneel beside me.

She doesn't want him to leave. What if *he* wants to stay?

What happens when he comes back and finds his whole world upside down?

After the near jump, Mom wouldn't let me out of her sight. She wanted to call for an ambulance, but Dad talked her out of it. He understood what had happened. "We don't want to draw attention to ourselves," he said, and promised her we'd call the doctor in the morning. I did my own part, convincing her that I was tired (true) and hungry (also true). The grilled cheese sandwich and OJ did make me feel better. So did telling them what I overheard at the gala and what I thought it might mean.

"I certainly wouldn't put it past them," Mom said, keeping her voice below the classical music.

Dad agreed. "Can't do much about it locked up inside, though."

So we waited all day for them to announce the end of the lockdown, but the broadcast never came.

Outside, the street is finally quiet. Inside, we're quiet, too. Dad pats my knee twice before pushing himself up from his end of the couch and stretching. He kisses Mom, who's dozing in the chair, and says, "Go to bed."

She yawns. "Have you been keeping an eye on Danny?"

"Danny's fine. It's late. Get some rest."

She squeezes his hand, and he goes down the hall. We listen in silence to the sounds of him getting ready for bed. "You scared me today," Mom says, her eyes drooping. Then she rests her head on her hand and sighs. "Wouldn't be the first time, though."

"Really?"

"Oh, don't play innocent with me, young man. You know you love giving me a heart attack every chance you get." She shifts in her chair and crosses her feet. Her voice is sleepy. "I remember when you were two. You were as cute as a button, running around the backyard with Holly. Aw, Holly." She puts a hand on her chest. "Miss that dog. Anyway, you found a stick and decided it would be really great to run with it in your mouth. Do you remember what happened?"

I cringe. "I fell?"

She slaps her hands together to show the impact. "Oh, the screaming. Yours *and* mine. You scraped up your soft palate pretty bad. Lucky that's all you did. And would you believe we caught you doing the exact same thing a week later?" She shakes her head. "I swear, you and your father. So much alike."

"You and I are alike, too," I say, setting my foot by hers. "Look. Same toes."

She scoots hers forward until they touch.

"I'm sorry I scared you."

"I'll live." She taps her foot on mine, then pushes herself up. I scramble to help her. "Are you sure you're okay?" she asks.

I hate lying to her, but it's for the best. "I'm sure."

"Then I'll see you in the morning." She lets me help her as far as the hall, then takes it from there.

I sit back on the couch and wait, looking at my toes, wishing I had time to hear all of her stories. When I'm sure they're both asleep, I pull on my shoes and sweatshirt, and slip quietly from the house. The way I see it, I have one last chance, and I'd better not waste it.

57

EEVEE

With classes canceled and students confined to the dorms, all I've been able to do since I got here is stare at the walls. I tried painting, but it's like the life has been drained from my hands.

Outside my window, campus lies dark and still. It's hard to believe there's anything bad going on at all. Kierland always has been its own kind of bubble. I watch for signs of life, then let the blinds slip back into place and flop onto the bed.

I miss the flame-haired girl, with her daring eyes. Is she still hanging in the gallery? I bet the Art Guild took her down. Too dangerous. People might see her and *feel* dangerous. They might ask questions or think for themselves. Anger flickers up inside me. I shouldn't have left her there.

Two soft taps at the door startle me. I rush around the room, turning all the paintings over to their safe sides, then pull my robe closed over my pajamas before answering.

Seeing him makes me catch my breath. I try to close the door but he stops it with his hand. He looks awful, like he crawled here on his knees. "I had to see you," he says.

"Why, so you can lie to me some more?"

"Please, just hear me out. There's something I need you to know. Then I'll go and you'll never see me again."

We stare at each other. My feet feel like they're bolted to the floor. He looks away first, up and down the hallway. "Please."

"You have thirty seconds."

He swallows and nods. "At the gala, I overheard Senator Hayes talking to your dad's chief of staff." Then he launches into yet another crazy story, this one about the government setting up a fake terrorist group to attack the city and make people so afraid that they'll want to sign up for Skylar.

"I can't believe I'm even listening to this," I say, pushing against the door. "You're delusional."

"It's true," he says. "Everything I've told you is true. Ask Germ. He and Danny were working for Red December the morning of the attack, but then we found out they weren't—"

"What?" My hand lets go and the door swings inward. "You're involved with Red December?"

"No." He holds up his hands. "The other Danny was. But what I'm saying is, Red December *doesn't exist.*"

"Unbelievable." My voice is loud but I don't even care anymore. "I'm sure the families of the people who died would love to hear that." I grab my phone and press the button to call security. Then I slam the door and let my forehead fall against it, my eyes squeezed shut, my fingers still gripping the knob.

"I'm leaving, Eevee," he says, his voice right there on the other side. "When they turn on Skylar, it'll send me back to my world. I've been fighting to stay here. But I'd rather be there, where I have nothing, than be here, where I have everything except you."

Shouting fills the hallway. I crack open the door because I have to know, but nothing could have prepared me for what I see. Danny's skin is pale, his eyes glazed, and he's trembling.

I can't take my eyes off him.

"This guy bothering you?" one of the security guys asks. The other looks like he doesn't know if he should tackle Danny or call for an ambulance.

"He . . . he's one of them. He's with Red December." My voice sounds far away.

Danny falls to his knees. His wide eyes stare unblinking into the ceiling. It's like he's possessed or something. He pounds his fist against the floor and the guards step back. Then he pounds the floor a second time and the trembling stops. He looks up, startled, like he's seeing all of this for the first time.

"Get back inside," the security guard barks.

I take one last look at Danny and press the door closed. Sinking to the floor, I listen to them struggle. A door slams. Everything goes silent.

He's gone.

58

DANNY

I bolt for the stairs, but the guards are right on my tail. Their footsteps pound above me, echoing through the stairwell. Where did they come from? Did Eevee call them? I throw open the door and run into the night, my lungs still seized with cold.

Visions of the other world swim in my eyes: lying on the floor of the garage at the foster home, clinging to the bumper of Brent's truck, wading through the mess of tools and tangled power cords. Danny's in bad shape there. Whatever's going on, if I jump now, I'll land in the middle of it, and it won't be good.

As if this is any better.

I race through the shadows, avoiding lit sidewalks, but I know they're watching. There's no hiding now. Like a huge hand, Spectrum has me in its grip. I run with everything I've got, but what I've got doesn't get me far. A mile, maybe two, down deserted streets, past empty neighborhoods and dark parking lots. Lost in a part of the city I've never seen. Each step forces the air from my lungs. I press forward through the pain, imagining them watching, from one camera to the next, seeing how long I'll last.

When they've seen enough, they swoop in with guns drawn.

As if I could put up a fight. My strength is gone. They have to lift me into the back of the truck so they can cart me off to wherever they lock up terrorists and boys who don't belong.

All I wanted was a crack at a normal life: hug my parents, have a best friend, get the girl. But I don't belong here, and this world knows it. Soon I'll be dumped like a defect and sent back to where I came from.

When they finally open the truck's doors, the city is gone, replaced by dusty roads and mountain foothills. Strong hands reach for me, pull me from the truck, lead me to a single-story building lying low in its surroundings. Amber lights along the path give hardly any light. The stars shine down on me, cold and uncaring.

One officer holds the door while another pushes me through. Inside, the fluorescent-lit hallways are stark white. As they're booking me, the cold returns and images from the other world flicker in my eyes. I see an unfamiliar room. It's messy. Moving boxes stacked around. Whiteboards with diagrams and scribbled words. WORMHOLE. EMP. GRAVITY. I see the other Eevee's face, close to mine, her lips moving.

The camera's flash pulls me back. The one with the gruff voice tells me to hold still. Another flash and I'm pushed into a room with white walls. Chains clang against the tile as they shackle my feet to the floor. Like I could run. Like I'd want to.

I have no reason to fight, no reason to stay. Time toys with me, seeing how long I'll last.

"Come on, Danny," I whisper when they're gone, my throat catching on the words. I can feel him there on the other side, a thin web between us. What is he waiting for? "It's your life. Take it."

He must hear me, because like *that,* cold grips my chest. My arms buck against their bindings. I force myself to relax, to breathe, to let go. Blinding white gives way to swirling dark. Pressure crushes down, and I'm falling again, leaving everything I love behind.

The landing knocks me down hard. For a moment I think I won't breathe, but reflex kicks in and my lungs expand. Oxygen rushes my brain. Blind, I reach out, down. Rocks? Gravel? I lift my face and blink the world into focus.

Her dark eyes peer into mine. But it isn't her. It's the other one. I look down at my arms, see the scars and know.

It's over.

My legs stumble forward, break into a run, carry me away into the night.

59

EEVEE

I've sat so long with my back against the door that I can no longer feel my legs. I imagine my body turning to stone, a creeping numbness moving up from my toes. If I wait long enough, it'll still my heart and deaden my brain. Then I won't ever have to feel or think again.

But a knock startles me, sparking life back into my limbs. I lean over, trying not to make any sound, and peer under the door. All I see is a pair of black shoes. They aren't Danny's. Security? They don't look like something a guard would wear.

The shoes move, replaced by hands, then eyes. I gasp and slide back. There's a harsh whisper from the other side. "Open. The. Door."

When I look again, it's back to shoes. Then the whisper: "Eevee."

I barely have the knob turned when Warren pushes himself through, closing the door behind him. "You're not going to believe this." He lowers his voice. "They arrested Danny."

"I know."

"You do?"

"I'm the one who turned him in."

He drops his face into his hands and groans. "No, no, no."

"He told me about Red December."

He looks up. "So he knows? Did he tell you?"

"Tell me what?"

In one long, breathless spiel, he recounts the same story Danny told, about Red December, the government and Skylar. Even the part about Danny being from another world.

"How do you know all that?"

"Because I know things."

"But what proof do you have that any of it is true?"

He pulls out his phone, touches a button and holds it out for me to read. "How about Senator Hayes being arrested on corruption charges?"

"What?" I grab the phone and read the news alert, my mind spinning. I can't believe it.

"Their whole scheme is unraveling," Warren says. "Get dressed. We need to go."

"Where?"

He walks to the door. "To get Danny out of jail."

"But . . ." Warning sirens sound in my head. "We need a ride. I'll call Jonas."

"No need," he says, opening the door. "He's waiting at the curb."

"Not a *spy* spy," Warren says, sitting next to me in the backseat of Jonas's car. "I'm just a guy with connections. I know people who know things."

"And you?" I ask, looking at Jonas in the rearview. "You're a spy, too?"

"Nope." He steers onto the freeway. "I'm just a man with a car."

"But you of all people could actually be a spy," I say. "You must hear everything."

He doesn't respond.

"When things started ramping up with Skylar," Warren says, "I knew I needed someone on the inside I could trust. I did some digging and found out the governor is the only Arizona official with his own driver. I pulled some strings and got myself a secure introduction."

"The castle." My head falls back against the seat. "You used me to get to him."

"Well, I needed a study partner, too. Wouldn't have passed that art history test without you."

"Liar."

He smirks.

"But Red December's been around forever," I say, still trying to wrap my brain around it. "They've even arrested members, haven't they?"

"It was all set up. Scattered cells of petty criminals and disgruntled kids enticed with bribes of contraband and promises of fighting the system. No one ever knew who was pulling the strings."

"Which are you? Petty criminal or disgruntled kid?"

"What do you think?"

I glance over my shoulder out the window. An SUV driven by Neil, the guy with black hair from the castle, follows close behind. Germ sits in the passenger seat. Warren said there are more helpers in the back, including Danny's dad. "I think after this we'll all be labeled criminals." I turn back around and my hands fidget. There's one question still unanswered, but I'm too afraid to ask. I don't even want to *think* it.

"Try him again," Warren says.

I sigh and dial Dad's number. It's gone to voice mail every time so far. I get ready to leave another desperate message, but instead Dad's voice says, "Yeah."

I sit up. "Dad. It's Eevee—"

"Honey," he interrupts, "I can't talk right now. All hell is breaking loose." And he hangs up. I set the phone on the seat.

"That's a no?" Warren asks.

"That's a no."

"Right, then. We're on our own."

●

It's an insane plan, and when they catch us at it, I'm going to hide in the corner and cry. Maybe the judge at my sentencing will be someone who was appointed by—and *likes*—my dad. I look at Mr. Ogden crouched beside me outside the Gateway Detention Center. The family resemblance is strong. "You believe what he said is true?" I whisper. "About being from somewhere else?"

"I know it is." His eyes are sharp but his voice is kind.

How is that possible? I think again about meeting Danny those three separate times. What if they weren't random? What if there's some force out there, pushing us toward each other? Or maybe something inside, drawing us together? Like thirsty paper pulling watercolor into its fibers, or a dry brush taking in ink.

"Okay," Warren says, joining us in the bushes. "Once we get the signal, we're going to have a very small window. Neil and his crew will create the disturbance and cut the power. That'll be our chance to get in, get him and get out. Remember, if they come after us, we head for separate exits. Are you guys ready?"

Ready? To break into a jail? How would I ever be ready for that?

I nod.

The jail is tucked away in the foothills of the White Tanks, about forty minutes outside of town. It's empty out here. And dark. We sit in silence—except for our breathing—and wait. Seconds tick by into minutes. My legs burn from crouching and my hands shake with adrenaline and fear.

Mr. Ogden leans over and whispers, "Whatever happens, I just want you to know how happy you've made him these past couple of weeks. Thank you."

I don't know how to respond. *You're welcome? My pleasure?* I settle on, "He made me happy, too," which isn't a lie. I don't think Mr. Ogden realizes we're here because of me. Because I turned him in. Danny sure knows that, though. I have no idea what I'll say to him. *Sorry* doesn't seem to cut it.

Warren's phone buzzes. What comes next is a blur of noise

and movement: a loud *bang* from the other side of the building, yellow lights flashing at the door, shouting from inside, then darkness and Warren yelling. My legs scream as I run behind them through dark hallways that have no end. I have no idea how we'll find cell 24 in the dark, but I trust Warren knows the way.

Figures run through the hallways around us, some shouting orders, others obscenities. I struggle to keep up, but my legs aren't as long or fast. Danny's dad looks back now and again to check on me, waving me on with his hand.

We turn down a hallway—the place is a maze—and Warren slides to a stop. He pulls out his phone and shines a light at the door: 24.

My legs shake and lungs burn. It takes him forever to get the door unlatched, but finally there's a *click* and he rolls it across, standing back for us to enter.

I step through first. The room is stark, empty. Danny stands against the far wall, his legs shackled to the floor. My shoes clap against the concrete, sounding echoes into the empty corners. Questions and apologies race through my mind. When I get closer, he lifts his face and I freeze.

It isn't him.

It's the other Danny.

60

DANNY

When my legs can't run anymore, I walk, but it's not like I have anywhere to go. My feet wander, shoes scraping the road, hands hanging limp at my sides. This body aches like every muscle has been pounded with a hammer. But it's nothing compared to the hurt inside. All the pain I buried for years lies exposed, sparking like a live wire. My eyes take in the streets, the signs, the lights and trees, but all I see is what I've lost. Every breath, every blink splashes another image across my mind. Mom sitting in the living room chair, sharing stories from our past. Dad with the ocean wind in his hair. Germ's crooked smirk as he rattles a can of paint. Eevee beside me in the grass. Eevee's hand in mine. Eevee's hair falling around her shoulders. Eevee's soft lips and dangerous eyes.

Being here is a slap in the face. A scab ripped off. I haven't felt like this since—

Light throws my shadow out in front of me and I hear the car engine, the blaring horn. I keep walking, though. Right down the center line. The driver swerves and misses. Taillights glare like angry eyes. Then it's just me again, in the dark.

I make a right, a left. The road turns to gravel and I pass beneath the iron arch. It's been years but I still know the way. Some things don't change, no matter how much you want them to.

The grass dampens the sound of my footsteps. I pass pinwheels and glass globes and vases of plastic flowers faded from the sun. Then I see them, and I sink to my knees. Even in the dark, I know what the grave marker says: PARKER OGDEN. REBECCA OGDEN. My fingers trace the infinity symbol between their names. All at once, the pain wells up. I raise angry fists to the sky and, with everything I have, break the night with a scream so loud I know my parents hear it, wherever they are. Then I fall onto their graves, my arms spread out wide to hold them, and I cry. Not just for them, but for Eevee and for Germ. For Benny and for Warren. For the hurt I caused others and the hurt done to me. For all the things wrong in the world. For nothing being how it should be. For love and the hole it leaves when it's gone.

I don't want to live here like this.

I don't want to live here.

I don't want to live.

Is that the answer? I turn onto my back and stare into the sky. Stars blur through my tears, swirling lights in the inky black. My breath catches; my mouth opens. I feel her next to me, her head on my chest, her voice whispering as she points out the stars of yellow paint above. *Isn't it amazing?*

"Yes," I tell her, my throat raw, my voice barely a whisper. "It is."

61

EEVEE

Jonas pulls onto the 303 and floors it. I hold the passenger seat headrest and watch the streetlights flash by. I've never seen him drive so fast. The dotted line on the road is almost solid. His face, though, remains calm, composed.

The roads out here are empty and wide open, and Jonas uses that to our advantage, putting as much distance as possible between us and what's going on back at the jail. When he approaches the Willow Canyon area, he slows to the speed limit, and soon we're but one of many cars driving along the freeway. Blended in. Anonymous. Still, we ride along in silence, Mr. Ogden in the front seat, Germ, Warren, me and Danny in the back. Somewhere miles behind us, four guys in an SUV are being chased south, acting as a decoy so we can get away. Will they make it all the way Outbound? I guess I underestimated Neil, with his slicked-back hair and too-cool-for-you attitude.

The road curves east, and Jonas maneuvers carefully through traffic. "We made it," Germ says, breaking the silence. "I can't believe it worked."

Everyone relaxes a bit, recounting what we just accomplished. I watch the lights play across Danny's face. They're the same eyes I gazed into, the same lips I kissed, but somehow it isn't him.

"We'd meet in the middle," he says, telling us his version of the world jumping. "Run into each other and sort of duke it out for who goes where."

"I bet you're glad to be back here," Warren says.

"Yeah." The way he says it, I can tell he's not sure. Mr. Ogden reaches his hand back and Danny takes hold of it.

When we get closer to town, Jonas slows even more. The city is still in turmoil and security is tight. As other cars are stopped and searched, we're waved on through. Soon we trade the freeway for major streets, then major streets for residential ones. The gates of Kierland Academy come into view, and Jonas steers the car through, passing the security kiosk with a tip of his imaginary hat.

We made it.

I lean forward to peer at the towering cottonwoods, the rising spire of Old Main. They're ghostly this time of night. Otherworldly.

The car veers right toward McConnell Hall. After much debate, we decided Danny would stay with Warren until I can talk to Dad about getting his name cleared. Warren put up a good argument that Danny's presence could jeopardize his contacts. I countered that it would raise a lot more eyebrows if the governor's daughter suddenly had a boy living in her dorm room, and that even with my personal security detail, Warren's room was far safer. I won, which was a huge relief.

Sharing my room with *my* Danny? No problem. Sharing my room with this Danny? I just . . . can't.

Jonas stops at the curb and puts the car into park. I make my goodbyes quick. A hand squeeze and smile with Mr. Ogden, a wave to Germ, a "See you soon" to Warren.

Danny opens the door to let me out of the backseat and we find ourselves standing face to face. Memories flood through me, bringing with them a sadness so big it'll drown me from the inside. He looks intently into my eyes, and I can tell he's wishing I were someone else as well.

For a second I think he's going to kiss me. And for a second I think that might be okay, but it isn't him.

It isn't him.

So instead, I whisper, "Stay safe."

And he whispers, "You too." Then he gets back in and closes the door. The car pulls away and I'm alone.

There's no sleeping after a night like that.

I sit at my easel, palette on my knee, and pull the spiral of a swirling tunnel from the canvas. My brush moves to match the motion in my mind. He said the colors were black on black, differing levels, swirling but not mixing. I layer the paint in ever-thickening swells. As I paint, I find myself moving closer to the easel, pulled in by a kind of vertigo.

There's another Phoenix with another me.

Is he with her now?

I load a smaller brush with a thinned mix of skin tones

and paint the hand reaching out from the center of the dark. As soon as I start it, though, I realize it isn't right. His hand shouldn't be reaching out with the palm down and fingers extended.

I scrape away the mistake with the palette knife. The edge scratches lines through the layers of paint. While I work to smooth the lines away, an image forms in my mind. I pick up the smaller brush and try again, painting a different story. His hand reaching, palm up, fingers relaxed.

An invitation.

62

Danny

Nowhere to land, I wander from one place to the next. Find some of my so-called friends. Crash on their couches. Eat their food and steal their smokes. It's cool of them to help me out, but for some reason it makes me feel empty.

I miss Germ.

A few of the guys ask questions. Where have I been? Who's that girl I've been hanging with? They must mean Eevee. Wish I had an answer so they'd shut up already. When I can't stand the questions anymore, I decide to risk a visit to the foster home. Grab some fresh clothes, maybe see if I can scrounge up some cash for a bus ticket out of here, to anywhere.

My feet have other plans, though.

They retrace the route I wandered the night I got back. Everything looks different in daylight. I take a couple of wrong turns and end up on dead-end streets or facing a wall of traffic where there should be a park. The sun's so bright it's blinding. Makes me realize how cloudy it is in the other

Phoenix. Too much gray there, too much blue sky here. Maybe there's a universe where everything is just right.

Finally, I find the right street, near the school, and the right house, with the gravel drive. I stop in the spot where I landed. Pick up a stone and turn it over in my hands. Why did I run? Freaked out, I guess. I push the gravel around with my shoe. Mac was there, and Warren, standing over by the front of the Jeep. Now that Jeep is gone. The windows are dark, the curtains closed. The only sign of anyone having been here is the deep tracks in the gravel leading from the stand-alone garage to the street and the sign on the front door that reads WARN-ING. THIS BUILDING IS UNSAFE. DO NOT OCCUPY.

Shielding my eyes from the glare, I try to see through the slit in the curtains, but it's dark inside. The front door is locked tight. My gut tells me to leave, but instead I look up and down the street to make sure no one's watching, then duck around to the back of the house.

There isn't a gate. Anyone could walk back here, like I just did. Weird. The yard is huge and empty. Patches of yellow grass struggle to cover the ground. A single orange tree with a white-painted trunk grows near the back patio. Rotting or-anges litter the ground around the well.

The back door's window is probably the easiest way in, as long as there isn't an alarm system. Guess it's time to find out.

I pull my sweatshirt off and am shocked—again—by the scars. How long until I get used to this body? I close my eyes for a second and try to remember what it was like being in the other body, but all I feel is anger. When I open my eyes again, they stare back at me in the window's dull reflection.

Can't even stand the sight of myself. I wrap the sweatshirt thick around my arm and smash my elbow into the glass. Shards rain down inside, leaving a hole large enough to reach through. I wait for the alarm, but all I hear is a dog barking somewhere nearby. I pull the sweatshirt back over my head, reach inside and unlock the door.

Whoever lives here—I'm guessing it's Mac—left in a big hurry. Either that or I'm not the first person to break in. The light switch doesn't work, but there's enough sunlight from the broken window to see that the kitchen cabinets and drawers are open and empty. Almost. A couple of plastic cups are still stacked in one, an abandoned straw in another. The air is warm and stale. A trickle of sweat runs down the small of my back. I open the fridge and close it quick after a blast of rancid air hits me in the face. Definitely left in a hurry. But why?

I step into the dark living room and stop. This feels familiar. Like I've been here before. There are dents in the carpet from furniture. A couch and chair. The four legs of a coffee table. Square shapes, too, but not as deep.

Packing boxes. Stacked three and four high.

This is the room I saw before I jumped. Eevee sat with me here by this window. Across the room were the whiteboards. What was written on them again? GRAVITY and something else. Come on, Ogden. Think.

My heart pounds as I move down the hallway. The house is so quiet it's like that dead feeling your ears get after listening to music too loud.

On the left is a room with an empty closet and closed blinds. A bathroom with checkered tile and a bar of soap still by the sink. On the right is a larger room with worn-down carpet. An office chair lies tipped on its side. I try the light switch, even though I know it won't work, then open the blinds just enough to let in some light. Something heavy stood in the corner. The outline forms a long rectangle, set at an angle. Mac must have spent a lot of time in here. Everything about the room says this is where stuff happened. The walls are scuffed and the paint is scratched. The closet door stands half open. I slide it the rest of the way. A few papers are scattered inside, all blank. I let them fall back to the floor and lean against the wall. This is useless. Whatever I was hoping for isn't here. Another dead end.

I'm just about out of the room when something under the chair catches my eye. Probably nothing, but may as well check it out.

I reach down and grab the wad of paper, then slowly open it, trying to be as quiet as possible. Pressing it up against the wall where the light is better, I run my hands over the wrinkles to smooth them out. My heart races as my eyes take in the pencil scrawl. *PORTAL?* is written in all caps across the top. Below is a sketch, an outline of a person. Scribbled circles cover the chest like someone traced and retraced the spot. Next to it are words written so sloppily and small I can't read them. Below the sketch is a bunch of math that looks like something straight out of Einstein's brain. I walk back to the window and hold the paper closer. One word pops out: *gravity*. And another: *electromagnetic*. The words from the whiteboard flash through my mind. WORMHOLE. EMP. Then I see what's been staring at me all along. Right there, under the sketch.

Danny.

I swallow hard and look at my name—his name—and the circles outlining the chest. Mac was trying to figure out how the jumping works. Danny must have come to him for help. And Eevee must have brought him here. Which means she knows.

Eevee knows.

I fold the paper and shove it into my pocket. Mac might be gone, but she's still here. Now if I can just get her to talk to me.

63

EEVEE

Keeping teenagers confined in tight quarters should be a crime.

Music drones through the walls of Warren's dorm room, loud enough to be heard even over the hum of his dampening field. Out in the hallways, students mill around, talking and laughing, throwing a ball, playing a guitar. Classes are still on hold, but they've lifted more restrictions. We're allowed to mingle in the dorms and dining hall, but we can only move between locations when the bell rings. Everyone is going stir-crazy.

Especially Warren.

There's a loud thud against his door. He looks up from the projected keyboard and yells, "Keep it down! Don't you know I'm doing important stuff in here?" He turns back to the monitor and groans. "This is never going to work. The modulating cryptography alone is making it impossible to hack, and that's just the first of several layers. It's like Dante's hell for hackers."

"If anyone can do it," Danny says, "it's you." He swivels in his chair to face me again. "Seriously. This guy must be a genius in every universe."

Every universe. I still don't understand it. Other worlds like ours. Same people but different lives. Part of me thinks, Yes, of course. Another wonders how it could possibly be real.

"So if the theory they came up with on the other side is right," he says, adding two wavy lines between the two horizontal ones he's already drawn on the paper, "then the opening occurs when the electromagnetic waves in both worlds collide. It's gravity, though, that actually pulls us through."

"And the whole thing was set off by—"

"The EMP the morning of the parade," he says. "The big bang, so to speak."

"Which everyone thinks was detonated by Red December, but Red December doesn't actually exist." I rub my forehead. Thinking about this has scrambled my brain.

Beside the diagram is the letter Danny—my Danny—wrote before he left. I read it again, imagining his hand forming each letter. On the back, he outlined our plan to take down Skylar. It's not much different from the alternate plan we're trying to get off the ground now.

Warren growls and pounds his fist on the desk. Danny mouths, *He'll get it,* but I'm not so sure.

I turn the letter back over and look at Danny's signed name. "What do you think he's doing now?"

"Missing you." He says it so matter-of-factly. "He doesn't have many good things going on for him there. I can only imagine how much it sucks to suddenly be back."

"What about you?" I ask, pushing the stories of the foster home from my mind. "Do you miss her?"

He doesn't hesitate: "I would give up all the good I have here to see her again."

I would do the same for him.

The knock at the door makes us all jump. "Did you invite someone?" Warren asks me accusingly, then turns to Danny. "You?"

Danny and I both shake our heads. Warren walks to the door and peers through the peephole. He turns around, a look of surprise on his begoggled face, then scrambles to transform the room back to normal. The lights change, monitors disappear, and suddenly it's just a regular—albeit *pristine*—dorm room.

He cracks the door and exchanges a few words, and in walks Dr. McAllister. I scoot the diagram and letter toward Danny, hoping he gets the hint to hide them away.

"Eevee," Dr. McAllister says, shaking my hand as I stand, "I wasn't expecting to see you here. I, uh . . . recently spoke with your father." He reaches past me. "Good to see you, too, Danny."

"You *know* me?"

"Of course." Dr. McAllister gives him a confused look. "You visited DART, remember? We tested the system?"

"DART?" Danny says. "But you don't work there—"

I can tell from his expression that he's mixed up his worlds. It's something I saw my Danny do often, though I didn't get it at the time.

Dr. McAllister clears his throat. "That's true. I don't work there anymore. I didn't realize it had become public knowledge so soon."

Warren moves his goggles up onto his forehead. "What do you mean?"

"I mean they didn't take kindly to my request to postpone the Skylar rollout in order to conduct further safety trials. When I told the governor I couldn't continue to work on the project knowing it could cause harm to people"—he motions at Danny—"Solomon let me go." He looks at me. "Sorry, Eevee. I think your dad is a good man, but on this he's very misguided."

Good man? I don't even know that. I hold up my hands and shake my head. "No need to apologize to me. I'm no fan of Skylar."

"That's good," he says. "Because I want to take the damned thing down."

A half hour later, the room is transformed back into a Temple for the Paranoid, and Mac is up to speed on our plan to fry Skylar.

"Those chips are brilliant," he says to Warren. "Remind me to give you an A."

"Thanks." The smile on his face spreads from ear to ear. "There are fourteen left to install, which shouldn't be too difficult a task if we get Germ involved. Eevee's got access to a car with executive privileges. The problem is getting everyone off Skylar's sights."

"Turning Knowns back into Unknowns," Mac says. "With most of the city registered now, a red X is going to show up like a big neon sign reading CRIMINALS HERE."

"Then there's no point," Warren says. "We're too late to even try."

"Not necessarily. There might be a way." Mac leans forward. "We could create false identities. Fake accounts linked to real signatures."

Warren's face lights up. Then Mac adds, "But to do that, we'll have to hack into the system. My access has been revoked." He gives Warren a stern look. "They'll revoke yours, too, if they catch you. Or worse."

He stands up and paces as he talks. The high-tech lighting makes crazy color shadows across his face. "Plus, if we are able to get in and change everyone's status, we'll suddenly be facing a ticking clock. I'd say twenty-four hours max before they figure out who hacked their system. I'm going to level with you. We're talking prison if we get caught."

"We've already risked that a couple of times," I say, joking. Well, almost joking.

"I say we get started." Warren claps his hands. He sits again at the keyboard and his fingers make a dull tapping on the desk.

Mac pulls his chair up beside him. "Finding a way through their armor is going to be the hard part," he says. "Thankfully, I built that armor myself."

Despite Mac's knowledge of the system, it takes them *two days* to hack into DART. Warren's voice on the phone Thursday afternoon is a mix of excitement and exhaustion. "Your twenty-four hours start now," he says. Then he yawns and adds, "If you need me, don't. I'm off to sleep like the—"

"Oh no you don't," I say. "Wake up, Sleeping Beauty. That was only phase one."

An hour and a call to Jonas later, we arrive at the first station.

During those two days of waiting, Danny, Germ and I created a map of the way stations and figured out the most time-efficient route for hitting them all in a twenty-four-hour period. With three of us—not counting Jonas, who said it wasn't in his job description—we decided that if we started in the southeast and worked our way northwest, we'd be able to get the chips installed before DART realized we'd pried off their back door.

Assuming it takes them twenty-four hours to discover us. Any less and we'll suddenly turn into red Xs on those huge DART screens.

Warren guzzles coffee while keeping virtual watch over our progress, checking Skylar stats and security bulletins and alerting us of danger. Meanwhile, Germ, Danny and I work quickly, moving through the city like ghosts, wearing the identities of people who don't exist.

Twice Warren calls us off moments from a drop because DPC has dispatched patrols. Each time, Jonas keeps his cool, rerouting us through neighborhoods until we get the go-ahead to try again. It's nerve-racking and costs us a lot of time, but somehow we swap thirteen chips before rush-hour traffic gets in our way.

Of course we saved the hardest for last. The final way

station is the farthest of all—way up at the northwest corner of the city, where the ocean meets rocky cliffs and the highway cuts inland toward Wickenburg. It's also really close to Wittman Air Force Base, so security's going to be super tight.

I sit in the middle of the backseat, with Danny on my left and Germ on my right. We ride in silence, exhausted from hours of driving punctuated by adrenaline-fueled chip swaps. The seats are comfy, though, and Jonas plays jazz on the car stereo. It could almost be considered a joyride if it weren't for the whole committing-acts-of-treason part.

"What's she like?" I ask Danny, my voice low.

He watches out the window and takes so long to answer that I don't think he's going to say anything at all. "She's smart," he finally says. "Sweet." He looks at me and adds, "Beautiful," before looking out the window again. "Those are just words, though. And all the words in the universe couldn't capture who she is or how I feel."

The car slows and Jonas pulls into a restaurant parking lot. The way station stands at the far end, exposed to the road. Not the best setup, but what choice do we have? The sun is going down, but the lights haven't clicked on yet. This might be our best chance, during the murky haze of twilight.

Germ leads the way and Danny follows close behind. I'm the eyes, hanging back to watch for trouble.

Halfway there, my phone rings. It's Dad.

Talk about bad timing. I've been waiting to hear back from him since our brief call before we broke Danny out of jail. I've been dreading it, too. There are things I need to ask him, things I need to know, but his answers could shatter the last pinnings holding my world together. On the third ring, I decide to take the risk.

"Hi, Dad." I plug my other ear to hear him better and pray a semi doesn't drive by.

"Eevee? Where are you?" The connection is glitchy and I hear voices in the background.

"I'm at school." A car honks and I cringe. "Outside. On the lawn with friends." I hear traffic noise on his end, too. "Where are you?"

"Eevee, I want you to stay right where you are."

My phone buzzes with a coded text from Warren.

3lv15 h45 l3f7 7h3 bu1ld1n6.

Oh no. Patrol on the way. I put the phone back to my ear in time to hear Dad finish his thought: ". . . even though I'm governor." I wave my arm like a crazy person, trying to get the guys' attention.

"Um, I gotta go, Dad. There's a thing. I'll . . ." Germ sees me. "I'll call you later." I hang up and run toward the car, looking behind to make sure they're following.

It doesn't matter, though. None of us make it. Two steps, and the parking lot fills with DPC squad cars and military personnel. I have just enough time to text Warren and strike the kill sequence on my phone before putting my hands in the air.

64

DANNY

Students stream out of Palo Brea High. I light a smoke and lean back against the fence. It takes almost a whole cigarette before I see her, walking with Warren. Her eyes catch mine. She grabs his sleeve and pulls him in another direction so she doesn't have to walk past me. Anything to avoid me.

I tried to get her attention in English class this morning. I wrote *TELL ME WHAT HAPPENED* on a paper and lobbed it over, but it bounced off her desk and landed on the floor. She stopped doodling and stared at the note. Then she packed up her stuff and walked out.

I pull the last drag from the cigarette and think about my Eevee. I miss her. Her smile, her eyes. Does she even think of me? Has she realized I was telling the truth? I hate not knowing.

As I walk, my eyes dart to the corners of buildings, even though I know cameras aren't there. Crazy how quickly you form new habits when your life is at risk.

Eevee and Warren walk through the park. I keep my distance, watching from behind trees and playground equipment. They talk. He picks up a stick and drags it through the grass behind him. She gestures to emphasize her point. He doesn't agree, but they keep walking, crossing over into a neighborhood. The sun hangs low in the sky, glinting bright orange off the windows. I drop back, hidden from view by cars and trees. Warren picks a flower and hands it to her, and for a brief moment, she looks happy. They say goodbye. He walks toward his house. She crosses the street, her head down, her book bag bouncing against her hip.

Her house is simple. Grassy yard with a concrete walk leading to the front door. Gray four-door in the driveway. Looks like in this world they don't have a Jonas to drive them around. No security detail either. She walks through the yard and goes inside.

Now's my chance. I'll just knock on the door and see what happens. Maybe she'll tell me what she knows. Then I can put this all behind me, raid my room at the foster home and take off for somewhere else.

65

EEVEE

I'm dead. So dead. My life is over. I'm done.

They surround us on all sides, taking cover behind car doors, trunks and hoods, like they're dealing with serious criminals, not some high school kids up to no good.

Up to no good? Kids spray-painting a building are up to no good. Kids trying to take down Skylar are committing treason.

Oh God. What have I done?

Engines idle and radios squawk, but no one moves. To my left, Jonas stands with his hands in the air. Behind me somewhere are Danny and Germ. I think. Maybe they got away. I don't dare turn to look. What if they did, though? Would they do that? Would they run and leave me?

My heartbeat thunders in my head, and my arms begin to go numb. One by one, the lights of the parking lot flicker on, and beyond them the neighborhood streetlights. What are they waiting for? I've never been arrested before, but this isn't how it happens on TV. They should be barking orders, closing in and slapping on the cuffs. Moving only my eyes, I scan the faces of the officers. Maybe one of them recognizes me. Maybe I should tell them who I am. Would they even listen? Would it make a difference? It's worth a try.

But as I open my mouth to speak, another car speeds into the parking lot. This one is black, unmarked. Executive. A door opens and out steps Dad.

He buttons his suit jacket as he strides across the lot, the sunset in his sunglasses. I don't have to see the rest of his face to know he's angry.

But I'm angry, too. My hands form tight fists and my fingernails dig into my palms. My breathing is shallow, my nostrils flared.

Red December doesn't exist.

The government is Red December.

My dad is the government.

My dad is Red December.

When he gets closer, he whips off his glasses. "Arrest those two," he says pointing behind me, not stopping until we're face to face. "What is this about, Eve?"

I dig my fingernails deeper. "Did you know about Red December?"

"What?" The question throws him. "Tell me what you're doing here."

"Tell me the government isn't behind Red December."

"This isn't about that."

"Yes, Dad. It is. Tell me the truth."

The muscles in his jaw flex. "There are a lot of things you don't understand." He takes a sharp breath and speaks in a calmer tone. "Get in the car and we'll talk about it."

When I don't move, he says it again: "Get in the car." He

reaches for my arm, but there's a commotion behind me. Voices shouting. A loud *bang*. Sparks fly from the way station control box and rain down from the power lines above. It all happens so fast. I duck low, fear catching the scream in my throat, as the parking lot is plunged into darkness.

But not just the parking lot. And not just the neighborhood. The entire *city* goes dark.

66

Danny

It takes all my courage just to knock on the door. Then I shove my hands into my pockets and stare at my feet. My brain races through what to say.

Hi, I'm Danny.

Maybe *hello*? No, *hi*. *Hi, I'm Danny. Do you remember me? Do you have a minute? Hello, my name is Danny. Do you know why I'm here?* Ugh.

As soon as the knob turns, all the words scatter.

A woman answers, pulling the door wide, a phone pinned between her ear and shoulder. Not what I expected. Her mom looks so different from the woman I met at the gala that for a second I think maybe I've got the wrong house. "Oh," she says, covering the phone, "hello." She looks surprised to see me. Or confused. She says into the phone, "I'll call you back, okay?" then holds the door open for me. "Come on in, Danny. Eve's in the backyard."

I take a deep breath and follow her inside.

The house is surprisingly plain. Not sure what I was

expecting. Something like her dorm room? But that doesn't make sense. She's not the same Eevee. She could be the total opposite, for all I know. Maybe she's good at math or into sports.

When we walk into the kitchen, her mom stops and turns. "Danny," she says, her voice low, "Eve hasn't really been herself since . . . you know. Go easy on her, okay? And don't worry, I won't tell her father you stopped by."

I don't know what to say, so I just nod. She turns and I follow her out the back door.

Eevee sits under a tree, reading a book. As soon as I see her, my feet stop. I know it isn't her, but my stomach twists and I feel like I can't breathe. I force myself to take another step and she looks up. Her mouth opens. Then, just like I realized she wasn't her, she realizes I'm not him. She closes the book with a sigh and sets it aside. "I'm sorry I've been avoiding you," she says, and it's amazing to me how much they sound alike. "I'm guessing you'd like some answers."

I can barely get out, "Yes."

She says something back, but I don't hear it because all at once my chest is slammed with cold. The force snaps my head up and blue sky fills my eyes. I make myself focus, though, to lock in on this moment, to be ready for whatever comes. The last thing I see before my eyes blink to dark is the surprised look on her face. Then gravity takes hold and pulls me away.

67

EEVEE

The night sky stretches like an ocean above. I imagine silent waves carrying me from deep blue to darkest black. With my eyes closed I can almost feel the earth spinning. Everything is adrift. Unmoored. Floating free. In the distance a siren wails. My fingers press through grass blades, searching for solid dirt below.

Warren got my final message. Even though I was sure we hadn't placed the last chip, I told him to pull the switch, to execute the program. I figured any damage would be better than none. What I didn't know was that in that moment, just before we were surrounded, Danny had made the last swap. As we stood with our hands in the air, the virus was worming its way through the system, generating some kind of surge that melted everything in its path. Spectrum. Skylar. It took down the whole power grid for a time.

And it was that surge, that electromagnetic wave, that opened the portal between our worlds one final time.

Or at least that's how we think it happened.

Laughter carries across the lawn. I look over and see the silhouettes of two students walking toward McConnell. I'm surprised more people aren't out. There are no cameras now. No yellow circles or red Xs. The gates are still locked—for our safety, wink, wink—but gates aren't a big deal when you know people who know people.

The Art Guild rejected my entry. They called it offensive, vulgar and inflammatory. Bosca won't even look at me. There's something satisfying, though, in knowing the paintings I finished for Vivian ranked best in show. Not that it helps her much. She's been absent since her dad was arrested—an event that prompted a complete turnover in Dad's staff. He couldn't beat Dad in an election, so he conspired with Richard to take him down from the inside. They were the ones who planned the Patriot Day attack, hoping to trip Dad up, cause him to make mistakes, get people to distrust and doubt him. It all might have worked, too, if it weren't for Danny and his trouble with electromagnetic waves. He turned up in our world right when we needed him. Random? Somehow I have my doubts.

A breeze sighs through the trees and I watch the branches sway above me. It's a beautiful night in an uncertain world. So many things remain unresolved. Did Dad know Red December was a government front? Yes. Have I forgiven him for that? Not yet. But we have an uneasy truce for now: I promised to give him the space he needs to make things right in exchange for him clearing the records of four kids who got up to no good.

Footsteps whisper across the grass, growing louder as they

approach. Then Danny leans over me, backlit and blocking out the stars.

The what-ifs still crowd around the edges of my mind. But when they grow too loud, I look into his face and a feeling of peace washes over me.

I'm not alone in this world.

And neither is he.

ACKNOWLEDGMENTS

All of the things they say about writing the second book are true and confirm my suspicion that we writers are a crazy lot. This is why I'm so grateful to be surrounded by amazing people who put up with, and even appreciate, my madness.

Thank you to Katherine Harrison for your wisdom, your patience, and your faith in me throughout this project. This book is as much yours as it is mine. Thank you to Christian Fuenfhausen and Angela Carlino for creating a beautiful cover and design. Thank you to Nancy Hinkel, Jillian Vandall, and the Knopf team for putting this story into the hands of readers.

Thank you to my agent, Josh Adams, for your support and encouragement, as well as the helpful reminders to breathe.

Thank you to James Sallis for taking me under your wing and teaching me how to fly.

Thank you to the Parking Lot Confessional: Amy McLane, Stephen Green, and Ryan Dalton. No one gets me like you do, grok?

Thank you to the Thursday-night crew, including Patricia Grady Cox, Marty Murphy, Nanor Tabrizi, Michael Greenwald, Jonathan Bond, Jonathan Levy, Paul Giblin, Hirsch Handmaker, Lynn Galvin, Martha Blue, Charles Dunham, Karen Reed, and Dean Burmeister.

Thank you to Dana Hinesly, Karen North, Trish Burdick,

Nannette White, Natalie Veidmark, Tim and Flower Darby, Cyndee Andrino, and Heather Wiest for your friendship.

Thank you to fellow authors Sara Wilson Etienne, Amie Kaufman, Shannon Messenger, Kimberly Sabatini, Allan Mouw, Jodi Moore, Jeff Cox, Chuck Wendig, Stephen Blackmoore, Beth Revis, Austin Aslan, Shonna Slayton, Bill Konigsberg, Erin Jade Lange, and James A. Owen for your support and example.

Thank you to the booksellers, librarians, and bloggers who've enthusiastically supported this series, including the incredible people at Changing Hands, the Poisoned Pen, and Mysterious Galaxy. Special thanks to Lee Whiteside, James Blasingame, Faith Hochhalter, Brandi Stewart, Jeff Kronenfeld, and Maryelizabeth Hart.

Thank you to my parents for instilling in me a love for books at an early age. Apologies, again, for the crayon scribbles in your antique-poetry collection. I think it was a sign. Thanks to my brother for all the Saturday mornings spent watching sci-fi movies and episodes of *The Twilight Zone*. I think that probably was a sign, too.

Thank you to Zoe and Cooper for your boundless joy and imagination. You inspire me no end. Thank you to my husband, Jim, for convincing me to give this writing thing a try in the first place. None of this would have happened without your love and support, not to mention your making sure the house didn't fall apart while I was on deadline.

In the words of Joe Banks: "Dear God . . . thank you for my life. I forgot how *big*. Thank you. Thank you for my life."

Finally, thank you, Reader. May you never stop asking, *What if?* And may you live a life your parallel self will envy.